RED LIGHT RUN

Linked Stories

BAIRD HARPER

SCRIBNER

New York London Toronto Sydney New Delhi

Scribner
An Imprint of Simon & Schuster, Inc.
1230 Avenue of the Americas
New York, NY 10020

First Scribner hardcover edition August 2017

SCRIBNER and design are registered trademarks of The Gale Group, Inc., used under license by Simon & Schuster, Inc., the publisher of this work.

For information about special discounts for bulk purchases, please contact Simon & Schuster Special Sales at 1-866-506-1949 or business@simonandschuster.com.

The Simon & Schuster Speakers Bureau can bring authors to your live event. For more information or to book an event, contact the Simon & Schuster Speakers Bureau at 1-866-248-3049 or visit our website at www.simonspeakers.com.

Interior design by Bryden Spevak

Manufactured in the United States of America

10 9 8 7 6 5 4 3 2 1

Library of Congress Cataloging-in-Publication Data is available.

ISBN 978-1-5011-4735-7
ISBN 978-1-5011-4737-1 (ebook)

Some of the stories from this collection have appeared elsewhere, in slightly different form: "Smalltime" in *Another Chicago Magazine*; "Patient History" in *Glimmer Train*; "In Storage" as "Intermodal" in *Tin House*; and "The Intervention So Far" as "Futures" on the website of the Illinois Center for the Book.

For Anastasia

CONTENTS

Beetles cont. – Order Coleoptera

Agrilus quercata
Common Name: Oak Slayer Beetle
Family Buprestidae

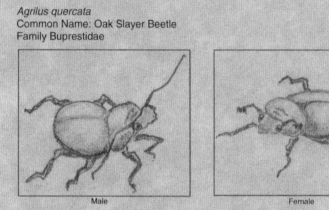

Male   Female

Elongate-oval in shape. Silver color on ventral and dorsal surfaces. Of the group of metallic wood-boring beetles known to undermine otherwise healthy adults, consuming heartwood, hollowing from within. Quite wary and difficult to collect. Look for rust-colored discharge that appears to "bleed" from exit holes.

Agrilus planipen

SMALLTIME

It's only an hour's train ride to Wicklow from downtown Chicago, but Bello tries to sleep anyway. If he doesn't get enough rest his hands shake, his conviction frays. But every time he closes his eyes it feels as if he's slipping underwater, cold and claustrophobic, a preamble to the chronic nightmare.

Bello reaches into his shirt pocket and takes the gold ring out, slips it into his mouth. He tongues it backward and pinches it gently between his molars. Warmly metallic, it pacifies.

A woman in a puffy coat in the seat beside him holds forth to the nun across the aisle. "Well, I happen to think," she says, "that original sin starts us off at a real disadvantage." She motions flippantly to the old prison sliding by outside the train's windows. "Speaking of sinners."

The decommissioned penitentiary looks like old prisons do, sober and monumental, a fortress of soap-colored limestone and barbed wire. Fingers of dying ivy keep wind-shivered clutch on the walls. The rust-stained sills below the barred windows stand out like swollen lower lips. Above the overgrowth and broken fencing a skeletal watchtower leans into the wind.

The woman in the puffy coat turns to Bello. "You know," she says, winking as she sips a blue sports drink from a plastic bottle, "the Soyfield Strangler did time there."

Bello has been advised by Virgil not to talk to anyone. He's been warned to be as unmemorable as possible. It'll keep his alibi secure. Virgil and the guys will tell the cops he was with them all day—"playing cards," they'll say—but if people start claiming otherwise, then the guys aren't going to let Bello take them down too.

"When they built the new prison up the road in Triton," the woman continues, "the Strangler went with it, along with all the jobs." She's younger than Bello, middle-aged yet somehow still in school. She's been talking constantly since they left Union Station, announcing again and again that she's a graduate student at Middle-Western. She's writing a thesis about the beetle that's killing all the oak trees. "Someone should've intervened by now," she says, her saccharine blue breath washing over Bello's face. "But now, of course, it's too late. Now it's just a tragedy."

I'll show you what tragedy is, Bello wants to tell her. But instead he waits for her attention to drift away again so he can spit out the ring and stow it safely back in his chest pocket. Then he puts his glasses on and says, "This is my stop." He gets off the train and walks north. The air, too cold for October, puts an ache in his chest. His hands feel bloodless. While he waits for a cross-walk signal to change, a woman comes up alongside him. It's the same woman from the train, except she has a purple jacket now.

She smiles, then stops smiling, reaches for him. "Are you all right, sir?"

Bello pulls away as she touches his shoulder. "Are you following me?"

"Why would I be following you?" she asks.

He can't smell her sports drink breath anymore, and her hair is a different color in the flat light. The walk signal illuminates. Bello stands in place as she turns and moves ahead of him. He walks behind her for a block before she takes a seat at a money-colored bus stop bench advertising a riverboat casino up the road in Triton.

Bello turns down an alley to get off the street, glancing over his shoulder as he rounds the corner. Alone again. The alley dumps him into an empty gravel lot with a view of the train line. He steps over a downed section of fence and walks along the tracks, eventually reaching the used car dealership owned by Virgil's half brother. It's called Woody's Hot Rods, but all the cars in the lot are used compacts with thin paint jobs and low tires. Grass grows through the pavement. The cinder-block building sports a pealing mural of a cartoon bird in a pin-striped suit. The sagging chain-link wants to guard something else.

"I'm looking for Durwood," Bello tells the receptionist inside.

The woman's desk is a car hood set on legs. The molded warp of the metal holds everything—her computer and stapler and pen cups—at tenuous angles. She points to the office behind her and says, "He's waiting for you."

"Come in," says a man in a padded swivel chair, not kindly. "Close the door." Durwood doesn't look anything like Virgil. This man wears a red tan on his face and neck. He sits behind a messy glass desk twirling a pencil with long delicate fingers. "You're older than I expected."

"I was told this is the place to get a cheap throwaway car," Bello tells him.

"Actually, that's *not* what this place is." The pencil flips up onto the desk. Durwood smothers it, brings it back into his hand, and resumes twirling. "It's a car lot. I sell cars here. I report my earnings. I keep my permits up to date. Once in a while, yes, I get a dope from the city who shows up because some wiseguy can't keep his mouth shut." He flicks the pencil back onto the desk, but doesn't retrieve it. "What I gotta know is, whatever you're into, whatever you're gonna do after you leave here, that it isn't gonna find its way back to me."

"I have cash." Bello pulls a wad of hundred-dollar bills from his coat pocket, the last of his worth, not counting the little extra in his wallet.

Durwood takes the money, puts each bill up to the light. "Okay," he finally says. "Fine. Go wait by the garage."

Around the side of the building, Bello finds the big segmented door. He sits on a stack of tires. He feels his age today, a peeling sensation on his heart. The big door grinds up into the garage ceiling to reveal a gray Ford compact, a mechanic in oily coveralls waiting beside it with his hand out.

"I already gave the money to Durwood," Bello tells him.

"I'm shaking your hand here." The mechanic's eyes are too close together, like two tarnished dimes pressed into the center of his face. "It's awful what happened to that lady. Was she your daughter or something?"

Bello shakes his head. "But I was *like* family."

"Well, I'm glad someone's doing something about it, if the family isn't."

Durwood bursts in. "Don't say anything to this guy, you dumbshit. Not a word."

"I was just shaking his hand, boss." The mechanic winks at Bello. In a sly new voice, he adds, "*It* is in the glove box."

"Didn't I say 'shut up' already?" Durwood shoves the mechanic aside and turns to Bello. "Keys are in the ignition, old man. Now get the fuck out of here."

1

The gray compact has no radio or heat controls, no dampers on the vents. The speakers are missing, the center console, the seat belts. There's an open cavity in the center of the steering wheel where an air bag once stowed. When he turns the key, the engine rattles to life and the cabin fills with the smell of burning motor oil.

Down the road, he pulls over in front of a locked gate, a shuttered mill cowering beyond. In the glove box, wrapped in a piece of newsprint, he finds the pistol. At first glance he mistakes it for a toy, it's so small. When he closes his hand around it, the hunk of metal practically disappears. He removes one bullet, tiny, like a filling from a child's mouth. An ancient memory rises, of the time he put his finger into the girl's mouth, her loose tooth tipping back, a thread of blood sliding into the wet canal behind her lip.

The gun is a sensible size after all, he decides, pointing it at the passenger seat, imagining what he might say before pulling the trigger. *Vengeance,* he'll say, *is served.*

He lays the pistol on the rumpled paper in his lap. Front-page news in Wicklow, Illinois, is a corn maze in the shape of the grim reaper. He wonders if the newspapers will understand that his need for vengeance was set forth by an original sin.

Bello tries to drive unmemorably, but people in Wicklow seem to have nothing better to do than stand around taking note of him, so he gets on the highway. After a few miles of corn and soy, a glittering billboard for the riverboat casino welcomes him to Triton. He has a while before it will be time, so he goes down to the riverfront where derelict shipping piers give way to a stretch of park space. The river is the color of green paint gone foul in the can. Across the way, the riverboat casino sits in dock, a massive pink hotel looming on the shore beyond.

Bello sits down on a bench beside a man with a duffel bag at his feet, a chain saw peeking out the open zipper. He wears a red sweatshirt with a logo of flames embroidered on the chest. Not far off, a midlife tree lies in pieces beside a hollow stump surrounded by an apron of sawdust.

"Nice day," the stranger remarks, a broad grin slicing through his face. "Tomorrow it's going to storm, but today? Today is nice."

Bello prefers not to talk to people anyway, but on this day his silence feels like a kind of rust forming on the brain. He tries to remember who he's spoken to today. There was a woman on the train, and again on the sidewalk. As he digs for their faces, though, he decides they couldn't have been the same person. And now this man is different too. Bello takes his glasses off and sets them in his lap. The world around falls into a lenient blur. "It *is* a nice day," he finally agrees. "I've been waiting for this day for years."

The stranger's smile turns dubious. "That's a bit dramatic."

Be unmemorable, Bello thinks, turning away. Without his glasses on, the nearest piece of the tree's hollowed trunk looks like a giant's ring. "These beetles," he says. "Someone should've intervened by now."

"*Agrilus quercata,*" the stranger says with an embellished accent.

"Pardon?"

"Oak slayers." The man coughs into his fist and spits on the ground in front of them. "They're here."

Bello knows he should stop talking, but his blood is finally warming and his tongue feels loose. Somewhere a crane keeps dropping its freight and the concussions feel like a second heart beating to life inside his chest. "There was an infested tree in our yard too," he says. "Or, it wasn't *my* yard really, but it was home." He stops, letting the silence take over again. In the distance, a barge the size of a football field churns upriver. "I was a handyman for a family in the suburbs. I lived in an apartment over their garage." Bello brings his hand over his shirt pocket, the gold ring thumping through the fabric. "I didn't have a family of my own, you see, so I was part of theirs." He pauses to work a knot from his throat. "But now I've lost everything."

The stranger nods as if this story is somehow familiar. He crosses his arms over his chest and the embroidery of flames flattens out into a picture of a tree holding bright autumn leaves. Below it are the words *Long-Lived Removal Services.*

"In life," the stranger says, "we don't usually get to see the trouble coming."

Bello isn't sure what to make of this statement. He wants to say, *That's a bit dramatic,* in the stranger's own mordant tone, but this day has room for only one confrontation. Instead he says, "Can I ask, do you know who the Soyfield Strangler is?"

The man's face turns suddenly restless with anticipation, his colorless eyes trembling, as if he's waiting for the punch line to a joke. He's delicately built, Bello realizes, beneath the thick lumberjack clothes, gaunt in the face, flesh drawn tight over the tendons in his neck.

"I'm asking," Bello adds. "I don't know myself."

The stranger's face washes over with something like disappointment, or relief, like a waking person throwing off the misgiven facts of a dream. He coughs into his fist again. "Sounds like a professional wrestler," he says, the smile slithering back into his jaw. He extends his hand and Bello takes it. The man's grasp is dry and stiff, a bundle of hard slender fingers. But when their handshake ends the stranger doesn't get up. His pale gaze moves to the dismembered tree on the ground, then to a copse of other oaks with red *X*s on their trunks, then up into the sky. Bello looks up too. Large dark birds wheel a hundred feet above them against a backdrop of dim brown clouds, a faint smell of tar on the air, freight pounding the earth.

Bello stands up. His eyeglasses fall to the cement and shatter.

//

On the drive to the prison, the nerves come on. A tingling in his arms and legs as though termites have gotten into the marrow. He stops at a quick mart for aspirin because he's heard it can prevent a heart attack. He opens the packet and swallows the pills before the kid at the register can even ring it up.

"Are you okay, mister?"

In the car again, his shaking hand pulls out the slip of paper with the killer's name on it. The pills lend no calm. He swallows a long drink of air and resolves that this is supposed to be the end, that it is finally time to surrender to this gathered fate. He looks at his hands, reads their palm-creased history, remembers again the feel of Sonia's loose tooth against the tip of his finger.

//

The town of Triton falls away in the rearview and Bello finds himself cruising through a wide collar of empty acreage—all prairie scrub and meandering ditch work. Outer fences guard inner fences. P.A. announcements on the wind. Bello's hands are so cold they can barely keep the wheel. He's afraid of losing control of the car, hurting the wrong person. A sign announces, GRASSLAND STATE PRISON.

A prison guard comes out of the hut at the main gate. "Can I help you?"

"I'm here for Hartley Nolan."

"Is he a prisoner?"

"He's being released today."

"I'm afraid there aren't any releases scheduled," the guard says.

"He got eight years," Bello says.

The guard leans back into his hut for a clipboard. "Nothing today."

"He gets out in four," Bello insists. "Today is four exactly."

"What's the name? Nolan?" The guard flips through more pages. "Hartley Nolan. Yep. I see the problem He's getting out tomorrow."

//

As Bello drives away, he can feel the aspirin eating through the wall of his gut, the stomach acids leaking out and welling up around his heart. This, he understands, is the sour creature he's become.

He parks in an empty lot near the river and closes his eyes, but sleep doesn't approach. Cold air blows through the door seams and somewhere a garbage truck wrestles endlessly with a dumpster. He draws the ring from his pocket and puts it in his mouth again, holds it carefully between his fillings. Metal against metal. He thinks back to the cozy little apartment over the garage. His heartbeat slows and he locates a full breath. The panic recedes. The familiar dread runs in.

Long before becoming a handyman, Bello spent years skimming product off shipping barges on the Calumet River south of Chicago, but he was always too careful about getting caught to make a real living at it. He didn't want his name in the paper. He was in love with a college girl back then, or a girl bound for college, still living under her father's roof. Virgil and the guys know all about it, his days as a crook. They call him Smalltime.

Before that, he was a harbor welder, which is how he still imagines himself, a strong young tradesman with a turned-up mask and a blowtorch in hand. Back then, all the ships in the harbor had women's names and they needed him. He made their anchors right, fixed their propellers. When he thinks back on it, there was a girl then too, a brat with a loose wet mouth and knee-high work boots the harbormaster brought in so they could all have turns behind the boathouse. Bello remembers hating her for some reason, for not disappearing after they'd used her up. Or perhaps it was that *she* had hated *him,* for his cold hands or his small pecker, or just for being last in line.

Once, he dove into Lake Michigan in January to repair the hull of a leaking freighter. He had to break up the ice just to get into the water, and this girl had been the one tasked with stirring the hole with an iron gaff while he worked below. It is the coldest thing he can imagine, those minutes underneath. Often, he dreams of this and the break in the surface has frozen over and the brat stands over him smiling down. He swims in circles batting the ice with his hands. The oxygen keeps running into his lungs, his blood turning to slush. It is the nightmare he goes to bed praying not to have.

//

At the pink hotel near the river, he gets himself a room. After putting down the deposit, he has forty dollars left to his name. The riverboat casino on the other side of the parking lot is free to enter, but they check IDs. Bello tries not to show his—be unmemorable, he thinks—but the rules are the rules. When he's through the gate, he takes out the money and throws his wallet in the trash.

The casino is exactly like others he's been to except this one is long and narrow and once in a while he swears he can feel the ship pitch in its moorings. Slot machines line the outer walls, and the open center offers blackjack, keno, craps, roulette. The din is monstrous, though in the middle of the afternoon there aren't very many people. Most of the tables are being kept empty, and the blackjack players have all been herded to the far end, near the bar.

Bello waits for a spot to open up at the five-dollar table. The dealer is a skinny kid with hair as red as his vest who wears the uniform like a costume. He's bored and courteous the way dealers are, but without the cold air coming off his chin. Something sparks in his eyes when a fat lady hits on a hard sixteen, and Bello can see how smart the kid is. He wants to know why the kid isn't in school.

"I wanted to ride the high seas," the young dealer replies.

A man in a Sox cap laughs hard at this to show everyone he understands a joke.

"Actually," the dealer adds more sincerely, "I dropped out." He pulls an ace of hearts off the pile and lays it on top of Bello's ten. Blackjack.

It goes like this for forty minutes, a run of luck like he's never had before. Bello plays it soft and wins two of every three hands. He plays reckless and takes three of four. He gets dumb and still breaks even. His forty turns into five hundred before the kid is replaced by a gray-haired woman who beats Bello seven times in a row.

The bar is separated from the gambling floor by tall glass panes that muffle the chimes of the slots. Horses race on the TVs. Bello takes a seat and watches the blackjack tables. He lays his hands on the bar top. They've finally quit shaking.

"Those hands hot today, sir?" the bartender asks.

Bello orders a whiskey on the rocks. As the bartender makes his drink, he thinks of those terrible minutes underneath the ice, the memory as fresh as last night's dream. And now this extra day demands that he endure it yet again, once more before it's all over.

"Before what's all over?" the bartender asks, setting the drink down.

Bello looks up, trying to retrieve his bearings. He can feel the ship tilt just so. "Someone I know is getting out of jail," he explains. "Early. For good behavior." Bello gulps his drink, feeling the liquor seep out the hole in his gut, his entire torso growing swamped. "I went up there today and waited for him, and do you know what they said to me?"

The bartender wags his head.

"He's getting out *tomorrow!*" It feels like he's delivering the punch line that the man on the park bench had been waiting for. But no part of this is funny. "What do you suppose that one extra day could be about?"

A grim smile creeps onto the bartender's face. "Maybe, for one day, the guy's behavior wasn't so good."

Bello sees the red-haired kid replace a dark-skinned dealer near the buffet. From the distance, without his glasses, they're just shapes and colors. But with the young dealer, Bello can *feel* the luck. He carries his drink out to the table, makes a quick stack of his chips, and pushes in.

"It's ten here, sir," the kid says.

Bello looks around. The other faces wait for him to understand.

"Ten *dollars*," says a man in a cowboy hat.

The kid's eyes study Bello, a quick scrutinizing glance like he thinks this bumpkin act is Bello's way toward the upper hand. But this isn't poker. There's no value in duping the rest of the table. Everyone's luck is his own. He pushes in five more dollar chips and the winning wave picks up again. The kid drops double face cards on him four hands in a row. When he finally loses, the cowboy screams, "I didn't think that happened to you, old-timer!" A large pockmarked goon with a name badge comes over to see if everything's all right. The cowboy grumbles that everything is just perfect. When the pit boss slides away, the young dealer resumes. The cowboy busts. Bello hits blackjack.

When the kid gets replaced, Bello leaves the table immediately. His forty is now over two thousand. He leans against a slot machine, finishing his drink. He watches the red-haired kid take over at a twenty-dollar table. There are only three other people willing to put twenty dollars down at a time— two men in gray suits and a greasy-haired mobster with reflective sunglasses. Bello sits and pushes in. He loses on a nineteen, then wins four of five. His stacks look absurd. He accidentally hits when he means to stay, and the five of diamonds makes his sixteen into twenty-one. The good fortune is overwhelming. It's as though he's left his own life and wandered into someone else's. He feels warm and buoyant and new, like a born-again believer stripped down to only his original sins. He separates three hundred dollars from one wing of his chip pile and pushes it to the kid's elbow.

"This is for your college fund," Bello says.

The dealer's face whitens. "I can't accept that, sir."

The mobster across the table pulls his sunglasses down his nose. "Take it, kid. This old man's senility isn't your problem."

Bello turns to the mobster, his hand settling on the lump of steel beneath the fabric of his pants. "You think I care what you say? I don't care at all. I've got nothing to lose here." He can see himself in the man's lenses—two withered twins skulking behind piles of wealth.

The pit boss checks in again. "Is there a problem here?"

"Everything's fine," the young dealer insists.

The mobster points to Bello. "This amateur's showing up the rest of the table."

A small crowd has gathered. Some young men in fraternity sweatshirts, a group of women in workout clothing, and standing near the dealer, Bello recognizes the removal services man from the park bench, his wide grin, his red sweatshirt. From across the table, without his eyeglasses, the autumn tree on the man's chest looks like flames again. The stranger's pale eyes lift and meet his own.

This, Bello thinks, is not being unmemorable.

The pit boss leans over the table, his neck folds biting a gold chain, his doughy hands spreading out over the felt. "Congratulations on your good luck today, sir. We'd like to invite you to join a table in the high rollers' club." He slides a gold-embossed ticket to Bello.

The pit boss sends the kid on break and calls in a new dealer. The disputed markers go back into Bello's stacks. A woman with a headset helps him carry his winnings to the window where the man behind the glass pushes a much smaller stack of chips into the metal tray. The markers are all glossy gray except for three stray yellow chips.

"What's this?" Bello asks. "Where's the cash?"

The woman with the headset smiles. "Don't you want to keep going?"

Bello takes the gray chips into his hands—each one worth five hundred dollars—and counts sixteen of them. They're a color he's never seen before, with greater heft, it seems, and a thick glassy varnish. A new class of wealth to attend the uncanny run of luck. "Keep going?"

"Keep playing," the woman says. "Or, if you're finished, you can cash out."

All around him the evening has brought on a horde of fresh faces, the shrill clanging of the slots overtaken by the lower, fuller sound of so many voices begging after luck. "Just these for now." Bello drops the three yellow markers back into the metal tray, and the man behind the glass replaces them with a stack of twenty-dollar bills. Bello fans them out, the smooth virgin bills. This was supposed to be the last day of his life, but now it feels like the beginning of something, the thrill of luck and money and the savory reek of the all-you-can-eat buffet making vengeance seem a distant, unlikely task.

The woman with the headset steps closer, touching his elbow. "Is something wrong, sir?"

"I could use a little fresh air," he says. "All this excitement, it's got me feeling . . ." The woman's eyes go dim waiting for him to finish. She seems familiar to him in this moment—her weary gaze and glossed lips—but the headset interrupts this impression, making her someone from the present after all.

//

Outside, the night has come on. Droves of gamblers pour past him at the entrance. Beyond them, the homeless shake their cups. He quickens his pace across the parking lot, hands palming the chips in his pockets, the pistol. He looks up after several minutes and realizes he's somehow missed the lighted concourse leading to the hotel. The big pink building floats in the sky behind him now, but when he walks directly toward it, he comes to a high fence between the two parking lots. He turns and shuffles along the fence, unsure now where he is in relation to the casino. Now and again, voices pop up and he wheels frantically to wait for a pair of old ladies to pass, then a bunch of college boys, a transvestite in heels. Each time, he finds his hand sweating on the pistol. He tells himself he's not supposed to care about the money, or about his life, but then there are steps behind him again, and he worries about losing his luck.

He steps up onto the narrow band of grass between the curb and the fence so his own footfalls don't obscure the sound of approaching footsteps, until he reaches a gap in the fence where a tree has recently been cut down. In the hollowed center of the stump, a hoard of shining coins glints dimly in the shadows. He reaches for them, then stops short, realizing that the pile of silver is actually a roiling mass of beetles.

He climbs over the stump to the other side, ducking behind a parked car to watch the gap in the fence, the black sky divvied into a thousand chain-link plots. His heart sprints. The wind carries the murmur of a distant bingo caller. Then a sound of footsteps again, a cough. A silhouette climbs over the stump, a thin figure in khaki pants and a dark sweatshirt with the hood drawn up. Bello presses himself against the car, palms the gun inside his pocket. The figure approaches, so close now that his mint gum is in the air.

Bello lunges from the shadows. "Why are you following me?"

Familiar hands push back the hood and the young dealer's face materializes, then his bright red hair, tousled now and wild.

Bello leaves the gun in his pocket. "What do *you* want?"

"You really blew it in there." The kid glances over his shoulder. "We could've gone on till the end of my shift if you hadn't dropped all that cash on me. You think the pit boss isn't gonna raise an eyebrow at that kind of tip?"

"So, you want the money after all?" Bello says. "Is that what this is?"

"I was thinking more like fifty-fifty." The kid shakes his head. "If you hadn't dropped that tip, we could've made even more than—how much?"

"I won eight thousand dollars," Bello says.

The kid puts out his hand. "Well, half of that is still *some*thing."

Bello stares at the open palm. "You think I was cheating in there?"

The dealer squints back curiously, as if he's trying to discern a joke.

"Is something funny to you?" Bello asks.

"You didn't see it, did you?"

"See what?"

The kid makes a flourish with his long fingers, as though sprinkling dust over his fist, then throws open the hand to show an ace of hearts in the palm.

Bello rips the gun out of his pocket, puts it under the dealer's chin. "I was riding luck in there, not some shady arrangement."

The kid raises his hands. "Okay, pops," he says, still smirking as he tips his head back. "Okay. I guess it's your luck even though I'm the one doling it out."

Bello touches the gun to the kid's throat for good measure, then turns and staggers through the lot. He pauses on the running board of a van to let his heart settle, every breath a taste of asphalt, car exhaust. A sedan trolls by on its way out into the world, its occupants still wearing their glassy gambling stares. He shakes the bullets out of the chamber and pockets them. He does not want to kill the wrong person.

//

Inside the hotel, he asks the desk for aspirin, but they only have Tylenol, so he goes to the bar and orders a whiskey. He pours it into his riddled stomach, and summons again the sour, vengeful man.

After he sets the tumbler on the bar top, he watches the vaporous outline of his clutch vanish from the side of the glass. "These hands were hot today," he insists. And for a moment he thinks he should go find the young dealer and tell him what luck really is. Shaking down an armed vigilante in a dark parking lot and coming out alive—*that's* luck. Or the removal services man in the park with his unsolicited advice. *In life,* he'd said, *we don't usually get to see the trouble coming.* But hadn't the trouble already come? Years ago?

A middle-aged woman on the next stool watches him swallow and breathe. She stinks of hair spray and vodka, so much perfume it holds a shine to her neck. She leans a bit closer and asks, "You win tonight, honey?"

Bello looks up, studying her blurred shape in the mirror behind the bar. "Tomorrow," he mutters, "is my day."

She swivels toward him, her knee-high boots connecting with his thigh. "Well, I'm more of a tonight kind of girl, myself."

She looks almost familiar, her tired eyes lolling in the sockets.

"It's always about tomorrow with you gamblers." She tips

back an empty drink. "But what would you be doing right now if there *was* no tomorrow?"

"Can you stop that?" Bello asks. "It's embarrassing, for both of us." In the mirror, he watches her absorb these words, her eyes narrowing, her mouth dropping open.

"This is when I throw a drink in your face," she says, "if I *had* a drink."

He digs into his pocket and drops the wad of twenty-dollar bills on the bar top. "Whatever she's drinking."

The bartender brings over a tall clear cocktail.

"That's better," the woman says, stirring her icy drink. "Now tell me all about your big plans for tomorrow."

Bello feels his heart peeling again, a textured sensation, as if the surrounding muscles are losing their grip, the chambers dividing. "I was going to kill someone today," he says, "but now I have to wait."

The woman's eyelids flutter sleepily. "You don't have to try to scare me, honey. I find the cash way more impressive."

Bello puts his hands on his thighs, feeling the contents of his pockets, the muted shapes of luck and vengeance. But there is room for only one confrontation. "Tell me something," he says, trying to sound benign. "Do you know who the Soyfield Strangler is?"

Her knee lifts off his thigh. "Okay, *now* you're scaring me."

"I mean it," he says. "Who is he? I want you to tell me."

She puts her drink down and backs off the far side of the stool. "I bet you think you're funny," she says. "But you're not. You're really just sick."

He watches her gather her things and leave, wonders if she's getting the police. Someone should, because a man who drowns in his dreams has too little to lose. Tomorrow, the people he met today will ask what they could have done to save a life, but their answers will be the same as his: *You cannot stop the past.*

The bartender looks up. "Pardon?"

Bello palms his tumbler, but his grip leaves no fog on the glass. He slides off the stool, all his cash still on the bar top. "For your college fund," Bello says. But the bartender is someone else of course, a big Irishman with a beard who twists his brow and says, "Are you all right, sir?"

Then the woman comes back into the bar, already having found a new companion, a big fellow in a blazer she leads across the room by the hand. They sit at a table by the window, the fat man's frame a dark blur in the foreground, the woman's neck shining open every time she throws her head back to laugh. From this distance, Bello can't tell if she's paying any attention to him. So he walks across the room and stands right behind the fat man, staring at her, waiting for eye contact. When the woman finally meets his gaze, her throat constricts.

//

Upstairs in his room, he undresses to his T-shirt and boxers. Loading the bullets feels like putting a thing back together, an easy repair, metal back with metal. He sets the gun on the nightstand and stacks the chips beside, pulls the chain on the bedside lamp. Sitting in the dark, he tongues the ring from its nestle between cheek and gum, slides it forward and spits it gently onto his palm. The wet hoop sparkles in the heavy dark. When he throws back the comforter and climbs into the sheets the bed is so cold he can already feel himself slipping under the water. His hands grow icy, his luck running away. He is unmemorable. He is Smalltime. He thinks: There is still tomorrow.

TIME AND TROUBLE

K ate eats this day's breakfast and reads its news. She takes a shower and gets dressed. She packs sandwiches for Hartley to eat on the ride home. The car is full of gas, the pantry stocked, the house spotless. All because this is the day her boy is finally being released. But then her husband comes into the living room saying something with the phone in his hand, and the day loses its meaning.

"I don't understand," she says.

Neelish's hands wring the phone. "I just called the prison to double-check the timing," he explains, "and they said he's not being released until tomorrow."

"Why would you call?" Kate demands, as if the act of asking has caused the delay. She thinks of the Greek myth, the one about the child abducted and taken to the underworld, to be released under the one condition that the mother not turn around to check on the child's progress on the long walk back toward the world of the living. Or was it spouses who'd been put through this mythic ordeal? She can't remember. Kate's field is language arts, but this fall she's a long-term substitute for a social studies teacher on maternity leave. All month it's been ancient Greece, the hallway littered with papier-mâché columns, Ionic or Doric or whatever they are. She knew the difference at one time, but now, with Hartley's days winding down, anticipation has made her stupid.

"Did I write down the wrong date?" she asks. Her absent-mindedness infects everything lately. She'll enter the pantry without a clue as to what she came to retrieve. Or she'll find herself walking down the middle school corridor past the sagging paper ruins, forgetting why she left her room to begin with. What period is it? How many days are left?

For almost four years she said nothing, but with the day creeping so close she couldn't not tell them about Hartley. As if she's proud of him now. Last week, during third period, she came out of a daydream about picking him up from prison, and the fifth graders caught her in this reverie, their eyes reflecting her own trembling excitement. "My son has been in prison," she announced. "He got into a car when he shouldn't have, but he's finally coming home, and now all that is ancient history." She could see their minds chewing on it, the smart ones already chasing down the truth.

Neelish puts his palm on her back. "Hartley can handle one more day."

She moves across the room to the padded seat by the window and looks out over the front lawn. She wonders if he'll stay for a while. for days or perhaps weeks. She's planned the sandwiches, and she's bought a large turkey for his first dinner, but beyond that his needs are unclear.

"We'll make new sandwiches in the morning," Neelish whispers. He's been whispering for months. If Hartley comes home tomorrow and isn't totally broken, if he can eat or smile or laugh, Kate has promised herself that she'll let Neelish take her to India this winter to visit his aging parents.

"I need another shower," Kate says and disappears from him without further explanation. Climbing the stairs, she feels selfish—this short temper of hers, these long showers—but there's too much conditioner in her hair, from an old brand she doesn't favor anymore, kept on hand to smell familiar for her visits, for when he comes home. She stands under scalding water for forty minutes, going over and over in her head the ways she might react if Hartley doesn't want to stay at home, or if he comes home and doesn't want to leave. She decides she'd like him to stay at the house for a few weeks and then re-start his successful life, to make himself an example to others. Then the hot water gives out and she rushes into mismatched clothes.

/,

At the bottom of the stairs, a set of matching luggage sits by the front door, as if someone is readying to leave. "Neelish . . . ?" she calls out timidly.

"In here, dear."

She finds him in the dining room sitting at the table, mugs of coffee set out and an open box of cake, something jellied and laced with icing, the kind Kate often considers buying at the supermarket but never actually does. Across from him sits Kate's daughter-in-law.

"Glennis?" Kate asks. "I didn't expect to—"

The girl rises from her chair, one hand held loosely inside the other.

Kate steps back and takes in her outfit. It wasn't that Glennis hadn't dressed herself up in the past, but in the years before Hartley went to jail, she'd been so drunk or hungover as to look limp inside her clothing, like a scarecrow rotting beneath its overalls. And before that, in the early years of their courtship, she'd been so casual with her appearance, her beauty squandered by an athletic, boyish style. But this version of her son's wife wears a gray cashmere sweater with a white collar sticking out the neck, a wool skirt straight out of the fall catalogs.

"I went to the prison," Glennis says softly. "I've had it on my calendar for months. But the guard said it's the wrong day."

"And then," Kate says, shuffling closer, breathing the air coming off her daughter-in-law, "you drove all the way here." The map in Kate's head doesn't add up. Wicklow, where Glennis has been living, is only a few miles from the prison in Triton, two outlying blips far beyond Chicagoland. How odd to have come all the way into the suburbs and not continue a little farther north and east to where she and Hartley had settled. Surely they still had *some* friends in Tower Hill.

"I let my lease expire," the girl explains. "The place I was renting in Wicklow was going to be too small for us. I've been in a hotel all week, waiting."

Neelish clears his throat. "I've suggested that Glennis stay the night, with us. Then we can all go over in the morning to pick up Hartley, together."

Kate seizes her husband's mug, drinking for a long moment. It isn't that she'd forgotten about her daughter-in-law, but she had quit considering the girl a part of her son's future. A friend of Neelish's who lives in Wicklow has kept them apprised of the rumors since Hartley went in—that Glennis was seen throwing up on the curb outside a bar in year one, that she spent a month of year two drying out in a clinic in

Minnesota, that in year three her father died and she quickly lost his house to the bank, and that more recently she'd been seen retching, again, in the bathroom of a diner, at ten o'clock in the morning.

"Yes, of course," Kate says, pausing to wait for a rebuttal. "Of course you can stay the night. Where else would you stay if not here?"

"It's decided then," Neelish agrees, ducking out to retrieve the girl's luggage.

Kate leads the way upstairs to her son's teenage bedroom. Pennants on the walls, rotten basketball shoes in the closet, an old kink magazine hidden inside a sleeve of printer paper. Standing there with Glennis, Kate has the urge to show the girl some of the things she's discovered over the years—the punched hole in the wall behind the Michael Jordan poster, the years-old package of Camel cigarettes (one missing), the page in the kink magazine where a bare-chested girl in a plaid skirt has a jump rope cinched around her neck. She wants to show Glennis exactly how well she knows her own boy.

Instead Kate says, "You look well."

"I feel well," Glennis agrees. "And I'm sober, if you're wondering."

"I *was* wondering, actually. I do think I have a right to be curious."

Glennis looks away, to a photo on the dresser from the first time Hartley didn't spend Christmas at home. Glennis's father had just moved back to his house in Wicklow, and as Hartley had explained it then, he and Glennis wanted to be there to raise the man's spirits. Kate hadn't understood. Or, she'd understood that her boy was a kind young man who wanted to ingratiate himself with his girlfriend's father. What mystified her was why Emmit had moved back to that wasted hamlet out in the cornfields in the first place.

"You must miss your father," Kate says.

Glennis's eyes hollow out and she lowers herself onto Hartley's bed, photo against her chest. "I miss everybody."

//

Back downstairs, Kate and Neelish wash the mugs and plates, trading glances and whispering to one another about their unexpected houseguest, until Neelish says, "Did you say 'lesbian' or 'thespian'?" Kate hasn't said anything close to either thing, and so leaves him to wipe down the counters on his own while she changes out of her mismatched clothes.

On her way through the upstairs hallway she notices the girl's suitcase has already been emptied, and that she's moved the green lamp to a spot by Hartley's bed.

In the family room, Neelish reads the paper. Glennis, he says, has gone to the store to buy some ingredients for a brine.

"A brine?"

Neelish looks up. "I think it's like a salt bath for the turkey."

Kate knows what a brine is. What she doesn't know is where her daughter-in-law gets off dictating the terms of a dinner in someone else's home. She heads into the kitchen, rifling through her cookbooks in search of side dishes that might upstage this brine. Or compliment it. She isn't sure what the effect should be.

"I think Glennis just wants to do something constructive," Neelish explains from the other room.

Kate rushes back into the family room. "But what is she *up* to, exactly?"

"They're still married," he says.

"I was still married to Hartley's father for a long time after *that* was over."

"You don't have to whisper, Kate. She's at the store." Neelish folds up the newspaper. "You used to like Glennis."

"When she was sober."

"She looks sober now," he says.

"I liked her *before* she became a drunk."

Neelish sets the newspaper aside and stands up across from his wife. "Kate," he says in a voice she doesn't want to hear, "their marriage is something you have no control over."

//

At the organic market, Kate moves down the aisles with purpose, swiping cans off the shelves, chucking potatoes into the basket, artisanal cheeses, a box of crackers with silhouettes of royalty clinking chalices. She hits the florist on Lake Street for gourds, dry wheat bundles, a wicker cornucopia.

When she returns home, she finds that the girl has cloistered herself in Neelish's office. A low babble murmuring through the closed door, as if Glennis is on a very personal call or rehearsing some kind of speech. Her daughter-in-law has always been a mystery to Kate. Before Hartley's incarceration, Kate often found herself in conversations with one person or another who knew of Glennis—of her gentle upstanding father; of her long dead mother, allegedly murdered by a serial killer—and when the gap in conversation arrived where Kate felt inclined to offer news about Glennis in return, she never had anything to say. Once, years ago, when pressed for an opinion on Glennis and Hartley's plans after their wedding,

Kate said her daughter-in-law was pregnant and intended to settle down as a homemaker. A total fabrication. She waited for this rumor to come back to her so that she could extinguish it, but nothing like it ever surfaced until years later when Glennis, drunk on Christmas Day, confided in Kate that a childhood fall from a motel room window had rendered her unable to conceive.

At the stove, Kate stirs the melting butter, adds the onions. Potato gratin requires enough repeated motion—thin-slicing the russets, grating the cheese—that it lulls her into a state of mindlessness. Undercooked, overcooked, gratin always turns out. An investment of time with a virtually guaranteed outcome.

Outside the kitchen window, Neelish is splinting tines on a broken rake. The leaves are still in everyone else's trees, but the white oak out back fell bare a month ago, a reddish brown stain bleeding down its trunk. Oak slayer beetles. The parkways all over town are lined with hollow stumps. Neelish has been threatening to rake for weeks, and now of all days. These four years are ending soon, and in moments like this one, with a red sun crashing through the empty branches above her husband's head, she worries that tomorrow will change nothing.

In the fridge, the turkey sits in a large plastic bag full of salt water, a great shivering load bullying the orange juice and milk containers. She finds the cream, pours it over the potatoes, and puts the gratin into the oven. Behind her, the office murmur changes pitch to a man's low crooning. She opens the door and steps in, turns off Neelish's talk radio, looking around to make certain no one's inside after all. Then she travels through the house, dusting manically, until she comes into the den to find Glennis on the couch, asleep.

4

"*Neelish,*" Kate calls from the back steps. "How can you be raking at a time like this?"

He pauses in the corner of the yard, casting a despondent look at the neat little piles he's constructed, as though he expects to be told to undo the work. Maybe he doesn't mind the thought. Anything to keep busy while the girl dozes on their couch.

"Has she been asleep in there all afternoon?" Kate asks as she approaches. "She's occupying our house like some kind of mopey teenager."

Neelish inspects the plot of unraked leaves at his feet. "She's just stressed."

"We're all stressed, Neelish."

He pulls the butt of his rake up under his chin. "She told me something."

Kate waits.

Neelish takes a breath. "She's pregnant."

"How long ago?"

"She's three months along."

"No, when did she tell you that?"

"This morning," he says. "You were in the shower."

"Is it Hartley's?"

Neelish nods. "But he doesn't know about it yet."

"When were you going to tell me this?"

"I'm telling you now." He waves at the house.

Kate turns to see Glennis in the window smoothing her sweater against her chest.

This is the problem with Neelish since Hartley went in. He'll clear his throat at the dinner table and say things like

"By the way, the Hollubs invited us to last night's Bears game. I told them no thanks. All that traffic and rain. But what a comeback. Then overtime. A classic! Oh well." They weren't so different—Neelish and Hartley—driven to secrecy by some misguided effort to protect Kate from her worries. She thinks of how Hartley used to cover for his father after their Friday nights together, claiming they went to the batting cages when the truth was that her little boy had probably been riding shotgun from bar to bar all night long. And years later, Hartley didn't even invite Kate to Glennis's intervention. Shortly after it took place, Neelish just happened to call Glennis's father for advice on purchasing new tires for the Camry. Emmit had said, "Don't worry, you guys couldn't have helped anyway, nobody could have," and then he went on about how Kate had raised such a fine young man. By day's end, Hartley was being arraigned on charges of DUI and vehicular manslaughter.

Neelish drops his rake to the grass. "You're not mad at *me*."

"I'm not?" says Kate. "Well that's a surprise, because I could swear I'm incredibly pissed off at you right now."

"You're mad at Hartley. You've stayed positive for four years, and now that he's getting out you're finally feeling some anger."

It does make some sense, Kate begins to admit, but then she catches Neelish eyeing his leaves, his excuse to let Kate deal with the girl all afternoon, and she discards this supposed anger, reminding herself, as she marches back across the yard and into the house, that Hartley is a fine young man who made one terrible mistake.

"Just a mistake," she tells the bathroom mirror. "Just one terrible, terrible mistake," she chants as she bows to the sink to press water to her face.

A knock raps the door. "Kate . . . ?" Glennis asks, her voice distorted by sleep. "Is everything all right?"

Kate looks at her red eyes in the mirror. "Yes, dear, I'm fine. Go away now please." She tiptoes to the door to make sure it's locked. She can smell the girl's cucumber lotion. She can feel the static off the cashmere sweater tuning the air just so.

/

By the time Kate's eyes recover, the dining room table has been set for three, the fine china on autumn-print place mats, the wicker cornucopia spilling its gourd bounty across the buffet.

"Neelish?" she calls out. "Did you do this?"

But as her husband comes into the room tucking a fresh shirt into his slacks, a grin cracks his face, as if this neatly dressed table has proven him right somehow.

"Sweetheart," he says, grasping her shoulders, "you need to relax."

At this, Glennis appears in the kitchen doorway holding plates heaped with a motley, derivative salad. The ingredients atop the lettuce are familiar leftovers from the past week's dinners, which strikes Kate as an intrusion, as if the girl has gone into the medicine cabinet and brought out the corn creams and fungal medications.

"I hope you don't mind," Glennis says. "I just threw together what I could."

"What about the gratin?" Neelish asks. "I thought I was smelling gratin."

Kate watches the girl absorb this comment.

"I assumed that was for tomorrow," Glennis says, turning to Kate. "Hartley loves gratin."

Kate takes a plate from the girl. "It *is* for tomorrow, dear."

Neelish's disappointment is palpable, a grown man suffering quietly but not subtly the torture of smelling caramelized cheese while eating a salvage salad. He tries to recover over and over, arranging on his fork a different medley of scraps, in search of some aggregate flavor greater than its parts.

Glennis must see this too, but she only smiles as she chews, winces, clears her throat to break the long silence. "So," she says, "do you think Hartley's going to make it?"

Neelish's mouth levers open.

Kate feels the blood run from her fingers, a chill crossing the backs of her hands.

Neelish says, " 'Make it'?"

"Hartley's *father*," Glennis adds quickly. "I meant to say, will Hartley's *father* make it, to the prison, I mean."

"Of course," says Neelish, breathing again. "Yes. Of course. Yes."

Kate puts her fork down, her appetite now fully extinguished. "No," she says. "I can't imagine Billy will be there."

"Right," says Neelish. "I was agreeing that of course she meant 'Will *Billy* make it?' "

Glennis sniffles, pinching the bridge of her nose. "I just, with Hartley on my mind, I'm sorry, I can't think straight." She shoves her plate away. "Jesus, this salad, it's terrible. Please, everyone stop eating it."

Neelish pushes his own plate away.

"The dinner is fine, dear," says Kate. "Neelish, honey, I made this food too, remember, the first time around. Let's just finish up."

But her husband is already on his feet, hands squeezing the back of his chair. He peers into the kitchen, the smell of gratin having grown clangorous. "I need some fresh air."

When the front door closes, a draft washes in across the hardwood. Kate wants to say something decent to Glennis in this moment, something that might wind back the years to when the two of them could cooperate in adoring Hartley.

They bus the plates, then wash them together in silence. Then Kate turns on the television, and together the two of them flip through channels, eventually settling on a show about a secret team of soldiers who pride themselves on their readiness. "We train every day for years," one soldier says, his face blurred. "And then, when something is asked of us, we retrain ourselves to the specific task. In that way, we are always ready and never ready enough."

In the window, Neelish reappears under a streetlamp looking hobbled. He's been jogging the block in his loafers again. Once, Kate followed him on one of these angry sojourns. It was wintertime, and she'd asked him not to go to Miami for a conference so that she wouldn't have to attend the Muellers' Super Bowl party by herself. He walked eight blocks in the snow, across a dormant ball field, and smashed tree branches against a concrete water fountain. Now, in the yellow glow of the garage floodlights, he doubles over with hands on knees, panting. Kate goes into the kitchen to see if there's a dessert to put together for him, but everything is for tomorrow.

When she goes outside to retrieve him, he's gone again. Overhead, the cloud cover has dropped so low that Kate can feel its pressure. She thinks of the dead woman—Sonia Lowery Senn—and of the wounded family. What must their extra night be like?

A light comes on above her, in Hartley's bedroom window, and Glennis appears, her body divided into pieces behind the lead grillwork in the glass. She looks doubtfully out at the darkening world. Then the light goes out.

//

In the morning, Neelish cooks eggs and bacon for them before excusing himself to the shower. Kate can only stomach the toast. In certain moments she feels like she's sitting across the table from her younger self. In others, she can't stand Glennis's chewing sounds, or the way the girl's necklace—a silver chain with either a cross or some kind of pagan rune on it—keeps slipping out of and back into the scooped neck of her sweater every time she dips to her plate.

"So did you find God?" Kate asks. "When you got sober?"

Glennis lifts her orange juice to her mouth.

"The last time I visited Hartley," Kate continues, "I asked if *he'd* found God, you know, in prison, and do you know what he said?"

Glennis puts her glass down, shakes her head.

Kate breaks off a wedge of toast and chews it carefully. Her teeth ache from grinding all night. "Hartley told me that the church services are run by a man who murdered all his children."

Glennis pushes her plate away, wipes her mouth. "The baby is Hartley's."

"Okay."

"It couldn't be anyone else's."

"I believe you."

Glennis looks at the chair where Neelish sat with her the day before. Kate looks at it too. All night she told herself it might be best if Neelish stays at home for this. Glennis too. The fewer people the better, for Hartley's sake. Months ago, she envisioned a grand welcoming party with refreshments and catered food. A criminal's cotillion. She even tracked down

Hartley's father. But that notion has eroded, so much so that she actually spent time last night talking herself out of hiding Glennis's car keys and sneaking away on her own.

Kate clears her throat. "Neelish said Hartley doesn't know about the child?"

Glennis nods.

"I don't feel good about keeping such a thing from my son."

"I don't either," Glennis says. "But I don't want to over-whelm him."

//

As Kate puts the key into the ignition, it seems certain not to start. This will be the thing that keeps her from seeing her boy for yet another day. And when the engine does turn over, she assumes it'll be the next thing—a sudden highway closure, a blown tire, an accident. With each passing moment in which calamity does not strike, the remaining miles become all the more precarious.

They take the tollway around the outer edge of the city, south then west, eventually onto a rural two-lane highway where the wind jostles the trucks. Neelish has assigned himself the backseat, and so Glennis buttons her way up and down the radio dial to find calm, inspiring beats. Occasionally a tune ends and a voice breaks in with report of bad weather, but after the first few warnings of evening storms Glennis clips the intrusions to a syllable or less.

They approach the exit for Wicklow. The blue Gas/Food/Lodging sign has spaces for six placards, but there's only a single marker for an off-brand gas station. As they pass the turnoff, Glennis sighs.

Several miles after Wicklow, they exit the highway and drive through Triton, then onto a stretch of country blacktop whose singular destination, as far as Kate knows, is Grassland State Prison. DO NOT PICK UP HITCHHIKERS signs float by. They pass through rings of barbed fencing, fields of yellowing prairie.

"Did you ever notice," Neelish says, "there isn't a single pothole on this road?"

They stop at the final ring of fencing, where a guard sits inside a glass booth. Beyond this is a fifty-foot corridor of chainlink leading to the building from which Hartley will soon emerge. Checking her watch, Kate sees that there are only minutes to go. He must already be out of his cell and through stages of processing. She imagines him walking down cinderblock hallways flanked by lawmen, guards who protected him because they knew he didn't belong among the murderers and rapists. He's left the relics of incarceration behind in the cell, his clothes and soap and books. As he walks toward freedom he must feel those dormant abilities that once served him so well returning at long last—his cordial speech, his boyish composure, the way he puts others at ease when money is at stake.

Neelish gets out to retrieve the sandwiches from the trunk. In the rearview, she watches him stretch his back, a bank of gnarled thunderheads on the horizon behind him. Nearby, a family of women and children sit on the tailgate of a pickup truck. In the space next to them, an old man talks to himself in the cab of a gray compact.

Glennis looks at her watch. But then there's a buzzing sound and movement behind the crisscrossing steel link. Doors swing open. Colors and shapes. Blue jeans. The inflated khaki torsos of guards. A tall inmate with a shaved head comes to the gate, staring out as a guard works with his keys. Behind him, Hartley shifts his weight from one foot to the other. The women and children rush across the foreground, but Kate hesitates, staying in her seat. It feels risky somehow. She doesn't want to clog her boy's release with an overexcited approach. The fenced corridor is so narrow that the guard can barely open the gate with this family in the way. When the door finally swings outward the scene crystallizes. Two men are being let out today, Hartley and this well-loved other.

Kate turns to look at Glennis, who has her hand on the door handle but doesn't open it. Let him come on his own. He'll recognize the Camry, years beyond its prime, retained for this day's purpose.

The door of the gray compact beside them opens and the old man steps out, unsteady on his feet. He surveys the scene at the gate, a grievous look bunching his face. The joyous family moves aside and Hartley comes through, a clear plastic bag hanging from his fist. The old man takes a few tentative steps out into the space between Kate's car and the gate. His hands jam around in his pants pockets. He squints. His shoulders droop. Kate wants to get out now, to tell the poor fellow that she understands the problem, that sometimes the one you're waiting for gets held an extra day.

Hartley walks by the old man, nodding as he passes, always such a polite boy. Kate rescans the lot for Hartley's father, relieved now that Billy hasn't made it. This boy is *hers,* and she takes all the credit for his humanity and good sense. This episode of manslaughter and whatever horrors the last four years have brought upon him are past him now, locked away for good behind the closing gate.

Glennis's door bucks open and she runs out to her husband. They hug without kissing. At first it seems odd to Kate that

they don't kiss, but as their clutch carries on and on she understands that a careful connection of lips would be impossible in
this moment of pure embrace. They learned to kiss each other
as nineteen-year-old kids, in a different life entirely. These are
adults Kate watches, hardened by time and trouble. She now
desperately wants them to come home with her, together, for
as long as they please. They can live in his bedroom. Perhaps
it's exactly what they need, to be teenagers again, to be cooked
for and to sleep away afternoons on her couch.

Finally a sliver of air opens between their bodies, and Kate
focuses on Glennis's belly, still small but not entirely flat. And
beyond Glennis, watching the scene with peculiar intensity,
the old man lingers restlessly.

Glennis leads Hartley to Kate, and as she hugs her boy the
anger breaks off inside her and dissolves. Neelish's arms close
around them both.

When they're all in the car—Hartley and Glennis together
in back, Neelish now in the passenger seat—Kate offers her
son a sandwich.

"What kind?" he asks.

But Kate has made every possible kind.

"Actually," the boy says. "What I really need is to pee."

A simple request. But as Kate puts the Camry into gear she
finds the old man standing in front of her, just a few feet off the
bumper, staring into the car, his hands still in his pockets. She
moves the shifter into gear, goes hand over hand on the wheel.

"It's okay," she calls to him through the open window.
"This happened to us yesterday. They sometimes keep them
one day longer. I don't know why. It's terrible."

The old man says nothing. He looks sick in the stomach.
Far beyond him, green thunderheads stir the horizon. He

opens his mouth to speak. His hand comes out of his pocket, a glint of metal, keys perhaps. He looks into the backseat of the Camry, crouching to see inside. Kate releases the brake and they're moving again, down the smooth blacktop. In the rearview, she sees the old man hobble to his car.

She pauses at the gate. The guard waves cheerfully as if this has only been an extended social visit. Unexpectedly, Hartley waves back. These are his friends now. Armed guards and cellmates. At some point he'll begin talking about his time in Grassland and this waving brute with the shotgun will be a character in one of his stories. The past will follow. It must. And the old man follows too, taking a right and then a left, holding firm two lengths back, his knuckles as white as open bone. And there's a look on his face, as if he's crying. He's gone insane with disappointment, made to wait an extra day for his own son. As Kate tries to lose him—left against the red arrow, an aggressive merge, a sudden exit—she imagines the old fool will take anyone's child, anything not to have to wait the extra day.

"Why are we heading to Wicklow?" Glennis asks.

"I really do have to pee," says Hartley.

Kate puts more weight on the accelerator. The old man keeps up. He holds himself tight to the wheel. He's right on their bumper as they brake for a stoplight.

"Is that guy following us?" Glennis asks.

Kate's afraid to turn and look directly. Neelish does turn. The old man is unfazed by the attention. She wants to call Hartley's father now to tell him it's okay he didn't make it to the release, and to ask him what to do about a distraught old man on their bumper.

"Don't," says Hartley. "Mom, you can't call the cops. I'm on parole. I can't deal with more badges already. I just can't."

Kate lowers her cell phone at the stoplight. She turns around to see the fear on her boy's face, to look directly into the eyes of the brazen pursuer. Glennis turns too, twisting in the seat, the belt drawing firm against her rounded belly, and Kate understands about the unborn child's own past, already mounting against it—conceived in prison, a convict for a father, an umbilical connection to a mother one weak moment away from bingeing on poison.

Kate looks forward. The light turns green.

PATIENT HISTORY

The last time her father traveled to Asia for business, Glennis threw a party at the house. A final stab at popularity in the waning months of high school. A dining room chair got broken and a boy threw up in the potted fern. Worst of all, the football whore, Astrid Sallingham, had sex with Tad Bucknell on Glennis's bed. This tryst left an invisible stain on the wall, which the full moon's light would uncover as a reminder that yet another month had passed without Glennis shedding her own virginity.

Her father, who wasn't due home until the end of the week, had promised to bring back a soapstone carving he said would dress up a dorm room perfectly. He'd filled out her application to the University of Illinois himself, even writing the personal essay—four hundred words on how having a mother murdered by a serial killer had defined Glennis's character. Or how it had *not* defined her character. She couldn't remember which, only that he'd used the phrase "for all intensive purposes." Her father was a lanky, forgivable man, eternally sunburned, with only three Korean phrases with which to negotiate the streets

41

of Seoul—*Good morning; I'm honored by your presence; I'd rather not go to another sex club.*

Staring at the stain on the wall, she wondered how it might really be, her first time, how it might've been with Tad, if only. And then, instead, her thoughts moved on to the man who sold trailers, of his stone-washed jeans and his chipped-tooth smile, of the way he'd roll up his T-shirt sleeve while watching football and rub the meaty blade of his throwing shoulder. The man who sold trailers was from Wicklow, where Glennis had lived as a small child, before her mother died. She couldn't remember much about the town, and whenever she tried to conjure it, her mind replayed the time when, still in the early throes of grief, her father had pulled over to steal a puppy from someone's front yard on their way out of town. "*Here*," he'd said to Glennis, dumping the animal through the car window onto her lap, tears wobbling in his eyes. "You need to take *some*thing decent away from this place."

Downstairs, Kidnap gazed out the window. The disheveled gray mutt looked desperate to be gone, but when Glennis opened the sliding glass door he ranged only a few feet out onto the patio to lie down and mope from there.

There wasn't anything to do in the suburbs in June with a geriatric dog to feed, so Glennis had taken up drinking, but with an eye toward recovery. She looked forward to becoming benevolently culted by the AA crowd or the born-again Christians, as it would be an opportunity to disavow old lives and maybe even recapture her virginity, assuming it would have gone astray by then. Her mother had been a drinker too, she'd heard, and judging by the incredible good time the woman appeared to be having in old photographs—always toasting the camera, always surrounded by boys near a keg, always smiling, smiling, smiling—it seemed to have brought her a level of popularity and happiness that Glennis still aspired to.

After a bowl of cereal and a juice glass of Beefeater, she put Kidnap in the Lumina and drove to the King Midas Mall. With the gin warming her cheeks and the dog smiling into the wind, Glennis made brave calculations for both their futures. "We'll be free and unattached," she told the dog. "We'll see the world!" In the mall parking lot, she made a sign reading, FREE DOG, JUST TAKE, taped it to Kidnap's collar, and let him out.

"You first, boy!"

/

The mall was the best place to spend the money her father left her because it promised chunks of time passing—long lines at the register, a three-hour movie, a giant wheatgrass smoothie. As she strolled past a store full of reeking candles and psychedelic tapestries, Glennis spotted a Lava lamp in the window and decided it should be hers. The icy blue blobs floating in the darker blue liquid would perfectly illuminate the aqua tones of the U.S. Navy poster on her bedroom wall.

"Good for a dorm room," said the stoned register clerk. He wrapped his hands in Grateful Dead T-shirts and lowered the hot glass tube into the Styrofoam packaging.

She always stopped by the Navy recruitment kiosk, which had been moved from its spot by the food court to a new place near the Twin Cinema. Her favorite guy wasn't working. Instead, Petty Officer Fontana stood in the vestibule peddling brochures.

"Don't need one," she said. "I'm already thinking of signing up. I turn eighteen later this week."

"You know," said Fontana, "you can sign up early with a parent's consent."

"I want to do it myself," Glennis said. "It'll be more official that way." Over the officer's shoulder, she noticed the recruitment kiosk was now sharing space with a press-on nail booth. "Why'd they move you to this end of the mall?"

"Vandals." Fontana's stern gaze tracked a stream of shoppers down the escalator. "We kept finding Taco Bell in the cabinets."

Glennis spun away, constructing an image of herself on a ship deck somewhere bright and exotic, a glittering port city on the horizon beneath the steel buttresses of America's long guns.

Across the vestibule, the football whore Astrid Sallingham stepped off the escalator and waved, boutique bags sliding up her arm. Glennis's naval reverie dissolved.

"Is it obvious, Glen?" Astrid turned to show her profile.

Glennis wondered if perhaps there'd been a nose job, a tuck of some kind. "What the hell are you talking about, Astrid?"

Fontana pressed closer to their conversation. His stomach whinnied.

"I'm pregnant." Astrid pushed her belly out. "I'm not sure it was worth it, Glen." She pursed her mouth, opened it at one end, and blew air into her bangs, looking like the exhausted mother of twelve she'd probably someday be. "Just one night of fun, huh. Oh well, in the end it will have been something great, I bet." She looked down at the bulge under her shirt, frowned, then marched off toward the Maternal Flame.

"Do you believe that?" Glennis asked.

Fontana tracked Astrid until she'd disappeared behind a

display of maternity bikinis. "Yep," he finally said, "I believe I'd have done her as well."

//

In the parking lot, Kidnap lay in the shade of the Lumina's bumper, wagging his tail at Glennis's approach. Scraps of the Free Dog sign hung from his maw. She gave him a good petting and poured the last of her water bottle into his mouth, then got in the car and sped away. In the mirror, Kidnap didn't chase. He only reared back and sat down, angling his head curiously at the sound the tires were making.

She considered this a preview of what it might be like to get on a ship for the first time and watch her father grow smaller and smaller on the shore. At this, Astrid came back to mind, the child in her belly growing bigger and bigger, then the memory of how Glennis's bed had looked after Astrid and Tad Bucknell had been screwing on it, the scrunched white sheets, the stuffed animals piled into a cairn-like sex perch. What had at the time seemed merely gross now struck Glennis as more cruelly ironic—that her virgin's mattress had facilitated a conception.

//

When she got home, Glennis called the man who sold trailers and said, "This is it, Rick. This is your chance. I'm saying I'd like to see you."

Rick LaForge was a high school friend of her father's, an old football pal whose name came last on the emergency contacts list.

"Glennis?" Rick said. "Is something wrong?"

"Not really *wrong*, no. But I was hoping you'd come check on me."

"But everything's okay?" he asked. "Are you sure? I promised your dad I wouldn't hesitate if you ever needed help, but, well, *do* you need help?"

"My dog ran away."

"Kidnap?" Rick asked. "He ran away?"

"I let him out," she said. "And he just ran."

He didn't speak for a moment. There was a clutter of voices in the background, a cell phone ringing. "It'd be an hour for me to get up there," he finally said. "If you're looking for someone to help, I have a friend who works in animal control near—"

"He's long gone, I'm afraid." Glennis made a sighing noise she thought might befit a woman in distress. "I could come down *there*."

"Oh, well yeah. You could do that. Except, I'm still not sure what—"

"I'm in a driving mood anyway," she said. "You're still in Wicklow?"

Rick smothered the phone and yelled at someone on his end about what time the inspector would have the report ready. "You don't mean tomorrow?" he asked, coming back on the line. "Hell, Glennis, you wouldn't believe the week I'm having. Everything's gone to shit here. How about the day after? Yeah. I can clear my morning. I'll buy you a good breakfast and we can set you straight or whatever."

"We should go to that place," she said.

"Which place?"

"That lounge at the pink hotel. With the big glass ashtrays."

"Okay, um, yeah, that one—" He broke off the conversation again, giving more orders. As Glennis understood it, Rick was a big deal when it came to mobile homes. He designed and managed entire trailer parks, each with an elaborate motif—an African safari park with a real tiger in a cage, a tropical paradise park with a wave pool and year-round palm trees. She'd seen the brochure for the one he'd built down in Wicklow too, a Hollywood theme called MovieTown set up on the grounds of an old drive-in theater.

"Then tomorrow," Glennis insisted, "for dinner."

"You mean the day after," Rick said. "For breakfast. Didn't we just decide that?"

Glennis drew her new Lava lamp out of the box, held the still-warm tube in her hands. "All right, it can wait until then." She hung up and made herself a drink. There wasn't any tonic left, but the gin went down all right on its own.

The afternoon grew sticky as clouds moved in and trapped the day's heat. She made dinner and another glass of gin, watched the scrambled porn channel, trying to figure what exactly she was seeing—a wagging tennis shoe, a mustache, a washing machine? When the bottle was empty, she went to her room and plugged in the Lava lamp. Lying on her bed, she uncrossed her eyes and stared at the Navy poster. The gleaming prow of a destroyer pushed through the ocean, its radar tackle climbing into the sky. Sleep approached, ushering her toward distant dreamscapes, but then she rolled over to find that the wall stain had reemerged, glassy and blue.

//

Mobile homes, Glennis had always thought, were for people who hadn't been raised in houses. But now, with the highway carrying her toward the man who sold trailers, certain old notions were coming up for review. She wondered if perhaps Rick lived in one of his own developments, finally deciding that he probably liked trailers enough to sell them, but not enough to live in one himself. That did appear to be the man's style, to dabble without making a commitment. The star quarterback, engaged several times but never married. And whenever he came to visit, he'd crash in the guest room only to pack up in the middle of the night and rush home. Restless Rick, her father called him. Or Slick Rick. Or once, when her father thought Glennis was out of earshot, Two-Chick Rick.

In years past, her father's old friend had broadcast a mostly platonic interest in Glennis, an innocuous brand of flirtation she took for generosity, or perhaps nostalgia, as she knew that he'd once been in love with her mother. But the previous October, she and Rick had run into each other at a hotel Glennis had wandered into while her soccer team's bus changed a flat tire in the parking lot. It was a large pink building near the riverboat casino in Triton, not far from Wicklow. When she spotted Rick in the hotel lounge, he invited her to join him on his side of the booth. They talked as she imagined adults did when children weren't around, with the casual swearing and weather-based cynicism. Rick stowed his gin and tonic between his legs and ordered a second one, and every few minutes he opened up his MovieTown brochure for cover so Glennis could lean into his thick chest and take a sip as his hand slid warmly down the small of her back.

Eventually, the big idiotic school bus pulled up in the barroom windows and the moment died. But now, as Glennis hit the outskirts of Wicklow, some remainder of those aborted passions reignited, and she said, aloud, "So what if he does live in a trailer."

/

Wicklow's town center consisted of a single intersection where a motel, a pharmacy, a bar, and a Planned Parenthood faced off at a stoplight. The air smelled burned and a wide curtain of smoke divided the southern sky. In the parking lot of Motel Wicklow, a tall teary-eyed woman in a Bears jersey moved car to car tucking flyers under windshield wipers. When the woman saw Glennis, she lifted her stack of papers and waved for attention.

Glennis hurried into the office, where the clerk offered a pitying smile. "Are you displaced by the fire, ma'am?"

"I'm just visiting," Glennis explained.

The man closed the reservations book. "I'm sorry," he said. "This week I can only give rooms to people displaced by the fire."

"I don't understand."

"It's the owner's policy," he said. "He's very concerned about the community."

Glennis turned and looked out the window. The troubled woman in the football jersey had gone back to distributing her flyers. "What kind of fire was it?" Glennis asked. "Did anyone die?"

The man waved off her questions. "What if we start over? I'll ask you again, and you'll try a different answer." He cleared his throat. "Hello there, miss. Are you displaced by the fire?"

"Yes," said Glennis, "I am."

"Awful thing, that fire." He spun around to rummage into a small steel cabinet on the wall behind him. "I'll get you a room right away."

"Is number eight available?"

The clerk looked sharply back over his shoulder, his face seeming to regret the consideration he'd been affording her. "No," he said slowly, not taking his eyes off her as his hand chose a key. "No, it is not."

The door to number twelve had a gap in the jamb where an old dead bolt had been kicked in. There were new locks above and below the damage, but when she pressed the door the entire wall flexed and a crack in the front window grew longer. Inside, the room met lower expectations—a bathroom recently cleaned by a coat of tacky paint, TV controller bolted bedside, yellow sheets full of lint and moth wings. The room must have been, she imagined, identical to number eight. Same clunky TV, same bland farm art, same feeble door.

/ /

At the bar across the street, Glennis ordered a gin and tonic.

"How old are you?" The bartender was a man about her father's age, with tight-cropped hair and a U.S. Army T-shirt tucked forcefully into his jeans.

"That's sweet of you to ask," Glennis said in the voice of an older woman. "How 'bout this shitty weather, huh?"

The bartender made the drink and brought it over on a battered cardboard coaster. "But seriously," he said, setting the glass just out of reach, "I do need to see some ID."

Glennis marched across the street to the pharmacy and bought the largest box of condoms, a variety pack with stallions all over the packaging. "Where's MovieTown?"

The elderly man at the register didn't look up. "Movie *what?*" He dragged a plastic bag over the box as though trying to catch it from behind.

"The trailer park."

"Oh," he said, nodding as if things were finally making sense, "the trailer park."

The flyer pinned to her windshield had a grainy photocopy of a dark terrier lying on a slightly less dark carpet. *Lost Dog*, it read. *Five Years Old. Answers to "Muggins."* But there was no phone number or contact information. She wondered how Kidnap was doing on his own, whether he was seeing the world yet.

In the car, she separated one of each color of condom and put them in her purse. The descriptions on the wrappings— numbing, ribbed, spermicidal—made promises about the experience Glennis couldn't fully anticipate. Pleasure and complication at once. She thought of Tad Bucknell, sweet simple footballing Tad, forever yoked to Astrid Sallingham.

She put the Lumina in gear and slid slowly through Wicklow—the rusted yards and browbeaten garages, the residents like loiterers on their own porches. Eventually she came to the small white house in which she'd spent her earliest years. Her father still owned it, renting to strangers. She could only vaguely recall living there herself—earthy brown shag in one room, a splintery deck out back. Most of her memories came from an album of her own baby pictures, her so-young parents with their infant child, forever yoked.

A proud-looking woman in jeans and a flannel came out onto the porch of the house, and for a moment Glennis felt a monstrous secret poised to reveal itself—that her mother wasn't dead at all, but living out the life she'd wanted all along, here in Wicklow with her first love, Rick LaForge. But then a fat man in a pit-stained undershirt came out onto the porch too, and the reverie melted, and the house was drifting out of sight, the smoke in the sky drawing nearer and nearer.

/,

Instead of trailers there were only rows and rows of scorched black shells, every single mobile home gutted by fire, some still smoking. At the entrance, a sheet of plywood had been propped up along the curb, spray-painted with the words MEETING TONIGHT! 6 P.M. MOTEL WICKLOW.

The old movie screen rose up at the far end of the lot, its corners coming unpeeled and smoke damage making a smudge up the center. Dozens of metal posts that had once held speakers stood stunned-looking among the blackened trailer carcasses. Their hulls had split open like torn Coke cans, the ravaged faces of toys and clocks and plates peering out at Glennis as she walked down the lanes between.

Coming around a double-wide, she saw a group of men standing together at the far end of the aisle. They all wore suits except for one man in tight jeans and a hard hat. They pointed here and there, made notes on clipboards, shook their heads, all parties arriving at the consensus that the trailer park had indeed burned down. To keep from being noticed, Glennis ducked into the double-wide. The smell of combustion still lingered heavily. Family possessions had merged with the floor, and the ceiling was cratered with the caramelized contents of burst soup cans.

"Glennis?" a voice called. "Is that you?"

She looked out onto the yard where one of the surveyors stood among plastic furniture melted halfway into the lawn. A tangle of charred wind chimes swayed in the foreground. As she stepped outside, her eyes adjusted to the light and Rick's face materialized under the hard hat. He looked taller somehow, his gut paunch had lifted into his shoulders, and his teeth held the sun in a startling way.

"Glennis," he said, "it *is* you. I thought we weren't meeting until tomorrow."

"I came down early to see the sights." She put her hand on his bare arm. "For nostalgia's sake."

"For nostalgia." Rick looked down, nudging something with his toe until a metal chain rose from the ash. "But what're you doing *here*?"

"I remember you talking about this place and I wanted to see it." She scanned the wreckage. "Do they still show movies on that thing?"

Rick looked up at the screen. "The whole place is burned down, Glennis."

"Right," she said. "I can see that. I mean, *did* they show movies?"

"What? Maybe. I don't know." He glanced at the group of men in suits who stood at a distance trying not to watch.

"These are all *your* men?" Glennis slid her hand up his arm, feeling the ridges of scar tissue on his biceps. "Very impressive, Richard." She tried to figure if he liked being called Richard. His eyes gave no indication. Dick?

"Look, Glennis." He pulled away from her touch, casting a frown over the scorched yard. With his boot he lifted the metal links out of the ash and the full length of a dog chain showed itself, extending to a stake in the center of the yard. "I'm having a hell of a week here, Glennis. Someone drops a cigarette and they blame the landlord." He lowered his voice. "These trailer people, let me tell you, they're just trash." His teeth had been bleached, Glennis thought. And capped. And veneered perhaps. They perched on his gums like Legos.

One of the suits cleared his throat. "Rick, we've got the fire marshal in ten."

"Tomorrow, then," Rick whispered to her. "At the hotel lounge."

//

Back in town, she parked in front of the pharmacy and walked across the street to the Planned Parenthood with the bright blue roof. Tall chain-link fences surrounded it. A security guard paced the sidewalk. The building had been a diner in its previous life, a greasy spoon she remembered eating at as a child, sharing a corner booth with her mother on a Saturday morning.

"I'd like to discuss my options," Glennis told the woman behind the glass. "Is there someone I can just *talk* to?"

Glennis sat down in the waiting room, which was like any other, except you could guess what everyone was suffering with. A freckled girl sat between her mother and grandmother. A blond girl with a man who might've been her father, or perhaps was not her father at all. On the form, Glennis wrote *Astrid Sallingham* at the top, followed by the number and address of a mattress outlet that advertised on TV.

When the nurse called her, she walked down a hallway into a room with two chairs and a small oval table. A poster of a woman cut in half hung on the wall, her organs in different colors like a still life of odd-shaped fruit.

"So you want to consider your options." The nurse's eyes lifted from the clipboard. Chains dangled off her glasses.

"My name is Astrid," Glennis said. "I'm pregnant by a boy named Tad Bucknell. He has a scholarship to Notre Dame to play linebacker."

"And this is a problem," the nurse asked, "that you're pregnant?"

"Actually," Glennis said, "I'm thinking of having sex for the first time."

The nurse tilted her head, the chains wobbled. "Do you mean for the first time since getting pregnant, or just for the first time?"

"The man I'm interested in," Glennis said, "he has these scars on his upper arms. Big self-inflicted cuts in the shape of my mother's initials. Her initials *before* she was married to my father. Apparently, back then, practically everyone was in love with her. But it's not going to be weird or anything, my being with this man. That's not the problem. My mother's been dead since I was very young."

The nurse blinked. "Then what *is* the problem, dear?"

Glennis looked at the halved woman on the wall. "I think there used to be a corner booth right in this spot. The pancakes were good, I remember. My mother used to bring me here as a little girl, just the two of us, on Saturday mornings." Glennis could almost smell the bacon in the air, the sweet tang of her mother's coffee topped off with a slug of bourbon from the flask in her purse. "You should probably know that she was murdered. Perhaps by a serial killer. The TV called him the Soyfield Strangler because that's where he left his victims."

The nurse eyed the poster too, as if curious what Glennis was seeing on it.

"But my mother wasn't found in a soy field," Glennis continued. "She was found in a motel. Room number eight. But there was a soy field *behind* the motel. Now it's corn. I checked it out on the way into town. Anyway, no one ever figured out if it was the Strangler or not."

The nurse swallowed. "I'm afraid I don't understand . . ."

"There wasn't a box to check for that," Glennis said, gesturing toward the chart on the nurse's lap. "Under patient history. But I thought it might be important."

"It does sound important."

"But really, it's the Navy I'm having doubts about. I've been thinking of joining up next week when I turn eighteen. My dad thinks I'm going to college."

The nurse's chains wobbled again. "I'm afraid I still don't understand."

"It's about options." Glennis stood up. "I suppose I'm still weighing mine. Thank you. This has been sort of helpful."

/,

Across the street, the displaced residents of MovieTown were streaming out of their motel rooms around the building into a dusty courtyard surrounded on three sides by the motel's brick walls. An old hot tub had been sunk into the center, big pale carp breaching the algal top water. Dozens of families milled about in front of a panel of men in suits. Still wearing his hard hat, Rick sat in a lawn chair with his arms folded across his chest, ankles crossed.

Glennis hung toward the back, finding herself beside the disturbed woman who'd been disseminating lost-dog flyers.

"What's this meeting about?" Glennis asked.

"It's about MovieTown, hon." The woman hung her hands

on the collar of her jersey. "Now we get to hear a bunch of lawyers explain exactly how far we gotta bend over and where they're gonna stick it."

Rick stood up and roused the meeting to order by clapping his hands. The adults took seats on the grass while the children ran off to play. Glennis hid behind the woman's teased-out hair.

"First of all," Rick began, "I want you folks to know that I respect you." Someone up front made a comment. Laughter sputtered through the crowd. Rick shushed them with another clap. "I respect you people," he went on, "but I won't be made a scapegoat for your shit-ass lot in life."

The crowd began shouting. The tall woman looked for someone to talk to, eventually finding Glennis. "When my husband hears this he's going to *kill* that man," she said. "He will. I won't even be able to stop him. I won't even *want* to."

Glennis felt a big shameless smile open across her face. She gazed past the woman, at Rick, and she could already hear herself recounting this crazed statement to him in the morning. She wondered whether they'd get the hotel room before or after breakfast, eventually deciding that Rick was the type of person who'd want to eat first. And what kind of room? A suite probably, with mirrors on the ceiling and a heart-shaped Jacuzzi, a bed that shakes.

One of the suits began to describe a timetable for removing the destroyed trailers and installing new ones as each family made a down payment, but the crowd wasn't hearing it. Order eroded. Rick wandered to the back of the makeshift stage and put his cell phone to his ear. Even from that distance, in the fading light, Glennis could see his new teeth as he talked, as he smiled. Who was he talking to? Another lawyer perhaps?

The fire marshal? But then he smiled again, in just such a way. A girlfriend? A fiancée? No. Just a friend, she assured herself. A guy. An old pal. And then it struck her: Rick was talking to her father.

//

She hurried out through the parking lot, across the street, into the bar. People she recognized from the courtyard had begun filling up the tables. When Glennis tried to order a gin and tonic the bartender offered her a weary smile.

"You don't understand," Glennis explained. "I actually need this drink."

The bartender's face softened. He said, "And I suppose your ID burned up in your trailer?"

She downed the cocktail and followed it with another, then another. She made small talk with a man who'd been in the Coast Guard, which was interesting if not at all the same as the Navy. "I want to see *all seven* seas," she explained, but when she looked up, the man had gone to the bathroom, or perhaps he'd gone home, which, she now remembered, was something he'd been trying to do for a while. The hour became dubious, the clock unreadable. Glennis turned to the bartender and explained that she was only drinking so much because she was thinking of leaving her boyfriend because he looked down on people who lived in trailers. She swore casually and complained about the weather, described what it was like to be pregnant by an all-state linebacker, how it felt to be defined by a serial killer.

The bartender looked at her fearfully.

"Yes," she assured him, "I'm afraid too."

"What is it you're afraid of?" he asked.

"I'm afraid my dog's never coming back." Glennis slumped against the bar, letting the room take a spin around her. The outside world had probably already destroyed Kidnap and left him to rot in some lonely roadside field. "But really," she said, "I'm afraid my Navy dreams aren't enough." These words—hearing herself say them out loud, not in the privileged confines of a doctor's office, but in that busy public space—felt nearly treasonous.

Glennis slid off her stool and tried to walk. She stumbled, caught herself on the pinball machine, then vomited on the glass. She assured the two men who picked her up off the floor that it was only morning sickness. But as they carried her across the street, she explained that she hadn't kept the baby after all. Her father couldn't know, she begged, and the Navy wouldn't understand. The two men dumped out her purse on the doormat, a mess of coins and condoms, a crumpled lost-dog flyer. The men keyed into her room and laid her on the bed. They pulled her shoes off and peeled her soaked shirt up over her head and took off her belt, and then they stood in the doorway discussing the possibility of terrible things happening to a girl they knew, until finally they pulled the door shut and their boots scraped away.

//

The sun rose in the cracked window, and Glennis woke into the nauseous despair that'd been bullying her sleep all night. Distilled junipers making a vile soup of her stomach. A brittle husk drawn over the brain. Cartoons shrieked from other rooms. Somewhere, a truck beeped in endless reverse. She showered and put on the dress she'd brought.

Outside, the tall woman sat on the Lumina's bumper smoking a cigarette. "Last night you looked more familiar." She surveyed Glennis carefully. "Which trailer was yours?"

Glennis moved past her. "I'm late for breakfast."

"Well," the woman said, "enjoy your pancakes."

Glennis looked back across the roof of her car. "What the hell does that mean?"

"Enjoy the pancakes," the woman repeated. "You're going to breakfast, right?"

"How do you know where I'm going?"

The woman ditched her cigarette on the pavement. "I didn't mean anything by it, hon. Just enjoy the pancakes. That's a pretty dress."

Glennis took a breath. She'd brushed three times, but a dry scum still lined her mouth. "I'm sorry for snapping at you," she said. "I'm just sick of this place."

The woman looked up at the big faded Motel Wicklow sign. "We all are, hon."

Glennis let the car's door and roof become crutches under her arms. "Which trailer was *yours*?"

"Mine had all the wind chimes." The woman tried to smile, but her jaw clenched and a frown ran in. "The one," she said, scrambling for another cigarette, "with the little black dog always chained up in the front yard." She finally found a cigarette, lit it, and inhaled. "I don't think he made it."

Glennis looked up at the curtain of ash still marring the sky. "I lost my dog too."

⁘

Glennis pulled back through town onto the highway, where she hung in the right lane, keeping her speed down, looking for the hotel. Eventually a salmon-colored building drew near. The parking lot looked wrong, but the big casino ship lay behind it on the river, and past the check-in desk it funneled into the same lounge from her memory. The bartender had a different face, but everything else—the woodwork and beveled mirrors—felt about right.

The bartender approached.

"Gin," said Glennis. "Just gin. In a glass."

She put money on the bar and lifted the drink to her face. The smell promised to trim the rug off her tongue, to make the trip home a little more fluid.

"If a man shows up," she told the bartender, "don't tell him I was ever here. Or, actually, tell him I joined the Navy." As she put the glass down, a shadow fell over her arm and she turned to find Rick, freshly showered, his hair still showing the comb work.

"*Who's* joining the Navy?" he asked in a conspicuous voice, his eyes worrying over the bartender.

She pivoted backward, into him, rising onto her toes to try to kiss him. He didn't move his head down toward her, or perhaps he'd moved slightly away, and her lips landed on the bony underside of his jaw.

"I am," Glennis said. "I'm joining soon, Richard. So this is your only chance."

He patted her shoulder, urging her off the stool.

"They have rooms available," Glennis said.

Rick carried her drink to a booth, not *the* booth, she noticed, but one along the same wall as before. "Glen, are you saying what I think you're saying?"

The condom wrappings came to Glennis's mind, a sharp anxiety about the language of sex cutting through the duller, broader grief of her hangover.

Rick urged her into one side of the booth, then put himself on the opposite seat. "You know, I was in the Navy. Petty officer first class." He made a salute, then sipped a tiny amount of her gin. "You're serious about this?"

"Very serious," she said. "Though I didn't actually ask if they had any rooms, but the sign out front said 'vacancy'—"

"About the Navy, Glen." He took a breath, a big windy sound that old people made when their patience was thinning. "The Navy. Let's talk about the Navy."

"Richard . . ." she said, reaching for him.

He pulled his hands back, hid them under the table. "Look, Glennis, about last fall . . ." His head tipped forward and he looked up through his eyebrows. "I'd had a lot to drink that day. A *lot*."

Glennis eyed her tumbler. Why hadn't he gotten his own? And the music wasn't right at all. And where were the big glass ashtrays? And Rick's teeth, there they were again.

"Look, Glen, what I mean is I'd love to, well, you know, with you, but it comes down to the fact that I can't pound another sailor. I just can't do it. It isn't right."

"I'm a woman," she said. "They do let us in the Navy now."

He brought his hands back onto the table and clasped them together. "I know that's how it might be these days, but it wasn't my experience. Call it retroactive Naval Code, but it shouldn't be yours either. Sailors don't plow sailors. It's the Navy, Glen, not some Army Reserve weekend warrior bullshit. You don't just try it out for kicks. You sign your name on the line and then they drop you into a trench for six months in a nuke sub and make you shine wrinkles off the cruise missiles all day and night. It's hard boring work, Glen, but it's damned worth it when you hear the deck guns laying waste to some godless port town. It's fucking glorious is what it is."

"Are we talking about subs or battleships?"

Rick unclasped his hands, seized her glass, and tipped the whole thing into his mouth. "We're *talking*," he said, alcohol flushing his face, "about the goddamn Navy."

The Navy. The Naval Code. Nuke subs. The goddamn Navy. These words he was saying were hers now—more hers than his even—and they meant something. They described who she was and would soon be. Codes and cruise missiles, sailors and submarines. These were the details of a life still waiting for her, a future coursing through her as she followed Rick out of the bar and across the lobby.

She felt suddenly lighter, as if afloat on her shoe soles, then floating literally, up three floors in the elevator, the buttons lighting up under Rick's touch, then his hand turning the knob on room 402, then his fingers prying up her bra. She lay back into the sheets, staring at the initials carved into his biceps, silently thinking Navy thoughts, letting him figure it out for her, the force and rhythm of the task. Letting him pull and push and grapple through this exercise, like a man trying to rock a vehicle out of the mud. Forward, then backward, then forward again, until all the false starts of her life so far seemed as impermanent as that hotel room, her life up to and including that sweaty grunting moment a thing she could now leave behind.

When Rick finished, she slipped out from under, letting him fall forward, face into hands. She went to the window and looked out over the river, to where the far bank eventually gave way to an ocean of soy. On the horizon, ash still rose from Wicklow, like an enemy port smoldering in her wake.

//

The Lumina lifted out of the parking lot and onto the highway. The gathering gin high merged with her hangover into a single, all-encompassing impediment elbowing out all thought, leaving Glennis with nothing but the wheel and the wind. And later, home again, as she lay on the couch watching the sun bloody the trees, a memory returned, a memory *of* returning, of her mother walking into that diner and sitting down beside her in the corner booth. A faint but true recollection, like a whisper on the ear. Like a scratch at the sliding glass door. Kidnap.

IN STORAGE

Hartley Nolan could see the future. He could see the coming ebbs and the coming flows of commodities markets. Somewhere it was snowing just the right amount, and the corn, not yet planted in the frozen ground, would have a good, damp spring as a result. A bumper crop was coming, an excess in supply. Somewhere else, a farmer's hogs were getting sick, a swine flu on the wind. The price of pork bellies would rise.

But this particular feeling, as he sat in his office in downtown Chicago, was different. This wasn't some hunch about wheat futures, but a more personal reckoning. An unshakable sense that his life was about to change.

"Dude, are you buying this or not?"

Hartley looked up from the empty space into which he'd been staring. Minutes had been lost to this intuition. Had he been asleep just now? Merely dreaming? He was awake now, surely, in his office at work, a manila file marked CORN IST QTR on his lap.

"I'm fucking buying it, dude. I'm thinking of buying it. I'm thinking of clicking the mouse. What do you think?"

Hartley's eyes focused on the man leaning into his office. A sweaty, red-faced person named Ken Locke, the very picture of where health can go during middle age. When Ken wasn't around, the other traders made fun of him by crouching into the pose of a wrestler and growling the man's self-appointed catchphrase, "Locke, stock, and buy low!"

"Nolan," Ken barked, snapping his fingers. "Earth to Wonder Boy. Where the fuck are you right now?"

Hartley blinked, scanning the red and green numbers on his computer screen. "Sure. Yeah. It's a buy. I think."

"So you're buying too?" Ken asked.

"Yeah. Or, I don't know yet."

"You just said it's a buy."

Hartley looked around for his coffee. Where had he put it? Then he couldn't recall if he'd even bought coffee that morning.

"Dude, seriously," Ken pleaded. "I'm sitting here waiting for you to stroke your crystal balls and give me a thumbs-up or thumbs-down."

Hartley glanced at the shelf above his desk, at the two Magic 8 Balls his old boss had given him. Around the office, Hartley had gained a reputation for hunches that paid off. A kind of corporate magic that no one actually believed in, but which everyone was afraid not to indulge.

"To tell you the truth," said Hartley, "I just don't have the intel on this one yet. I haven't had the time to research it."

Ken grappled his chin. "Fuck the intel, Nolan. I've got intel up to my ass. All week my intel's been getting me fucked. I'm riding instinct this time. Your instinct."

Hartley studied the man's reddening face. This was how it went for people in his business. Someone like Ken Locke came into your office one morning looking a little more unhealthy than usual, a little more stressed, a line of sweat on the upper lip, an itch in the left shoulder. Then you'd take a sip of coffee and suddenly the guy would be on the floor clutching his heart. Dead before the paramedics could arrive. Either that or your boss threw himself in front of a commuter train. That happened too. And in the wake of such events, others would see the light and say, That's enough, quit. A wake-up call. Life is precious. Stop tormenting yourself fourteen hours a day over the price of soybeans.

"Nooo-laaan . . ."

"Did Miguel go out for coffee yet?" Hartley asked.

"Who?"

"The intern."

Ken Locke's hands balled into fists. "Dude, what the f—"

"Ken, I really don't know what to tell you. My hunch is that I haven't done the research on this one. So I guess it's not a buy."

Ken Locke's face took a darker shade, then smoothed and lightened. His fists slowly unfurled. "Now I read you, Wonder Boy," he said, nodding slyly. "I'm hearing 'sell' loud and clear now. Your crystal balls have spoken, young buck." The man backed slowly out of Hartley's office, humping the air as he went.

Hartley looked down at the floor, at the space onto which he'd been sure Ken Locke was going to collapse. He looked around for his coffee. The feeling returned. He couldn't explain it.

"I don't understand," said Glennis. "Are you saying you want to quit?" It was midday now. He'd found his coffee around the corner, in a Dunkin' Donuts. But then he'd kept walking to the train station, then home to Tower Hill, where he found his wife sitting in the breakfast nook reading a novel with a glass of white wine. "I thought you loved your job."

"I'm just saying I had this really weird feeling," he told her. "I don't know what to call it. It was subtle, but huge. Like a—"

"A hunch?"

"It wasn't about work stuff. It was about me. Like a doomed feeling."

Glennis put her novel down. The cover had a collage of images—a submarine, a sleeping baby, a row of green digital numbers frozen at 00:01. Her eyes watched him over the rim of her glass as she sipped. "A doomed feeling, huh."

"Do you always have wine with lunch?" he asked.

"I haven't had lunch yet," she said, getting up. "Do you want a sandwich?" She got a second glass out of the cupboard and returned to the breakfast nook.

"Ken came into my office and I swear his heart was going to explode, right there in front of me. I thought I was witnessing his final moments."

"Doesn't sound all that subtle if Ken Locke was involved." She poured more wine into her glass, then began to pour into his, but he waved her off.

"It sounds like you could use a drink," she said.

"White wine makes me foggy."

"Everything makes you foggy, Hartley. That's the point."

"But really," he continued, "this was happening before Ken even came in."

Glennis tipped his splash of wine into her own glass. "Remember that dream you had about your dad living in a storage container? And the very next day that postcard from him came in the mail?"

"That was real," said Hartley. "He actually lived in one of those things for a time when I was a kid."

"I know," she said. "But a few years ago you dreamed about him, and then the postcard arrived the very next day. It was weird."

Hartley pinched his nose. "This morning's thing was heavier than that."

"I'll call your mom," said Glennis. "Make sure everyone's all right."

"You'll call my *mom*?"

"What? Why'd you say it that way?"

"When have you ever called my mom?"

"You're using the word *doom*, Hartley. I'm trying to take you seriously." Glennis had always believed in his ability to see the future. When they'd first met as nineteen-year-olds on spring break, he'd told her how it would go between them, how they were meant to be. After just a night and a day together, he'd laid it out for her in a diner two hours before his flight back to Chicago—time apart to let the heart grow even fonder, the drives he'd make to see her down in Champaign on weekends, the engagement after college, the marriage. At the time, she'd seemed to think he was being superlative, just a boy in lust. But over the years she'd come to believe in his foresight so sincerely that she'd stopped asking him the big questions about their own prospects. She was content with him applying it for the sake of making a little money, but he had the sense that, if times grew desperate enough and if a question were truly worthy, she might eventually call on him for one crucial prediction.

To Hartley, though, the ability to read the future was just a matter of understanding the past. Research plus intuition equals success. But there it was again, that look in her eyes, that sauced melancholic twinkle. She slid out of the nook and dipped to him to lay a wet kiss on his mouth. A sweet boozy mix of lip gloss, white wine, and a trace of something harder, not even on her lips so much as *in* them. When she pressed closer to him—a second, deeper kiss, her hand sliding down the side of his neck, dipping into his collar—he was reminded of the way she smelled in college, the honeyed bouquet of her flesh pickled by an all-night binge.

He reached for her, his hand running up the back of her shirt, their mouths opening on one another, the doom drifting away, his mind clearing, making space only for her.

//

He begins to wake, swimming to the surface of this dream, flavors of wine and lip gloss pooling in his mouth, until finally he emerges into the concrete bunk room that is still his home. A convicted rapist snores peacefully on the cot below. It is the middle of the night before the day on which he's scheduled for release. There is no clock to tell him the time, no window to carry the dawn light into his cell. The new day, with each dream, with each waking, refuses to arrive. The future stalls. The breaths of the monster in the lower cot count the seconds in reverse. Time backpedals. The past sits on its haunches in the predawn black of his cell. He can hear its slow breathing, its dark mouth consuming the future. The day won't arrive and he can't envision it. He doesn't know who will be there to pick him up. His mother will be there, but will his father? Will his wife? He closes his eyes and swims into a darker place. Into the mouth of the beast. Who will come and where will they take him? Where is home now? He squeezes his eyelids tighter, swims deeper into the past, to a time when his father had no place to live, evicted from home and marriage.

/,

"What do you think of my new digs?" he asked Hartley as they pulled up alongside the shipping container that was his father's new home. The long steel box was set off on its own away from the hundreds of other stacked containers in the shipping yard along the concrete shore of the canal.

"Riverfront property," his father declared, pointing to the spot on the freight container below the words *Lu Kang Intermodal* where someone had spray-painted a picture of a naked woman with bottle caps over her eyes. "But of course your mother," he added, "isn't to know that I'm living in storage."

They set out in search of what his father called "bach-pad essentials," down a street full of pawnshops Hartley knew well. The main showroom of Mel's Second Hand sold used housewares, greasy tools, stolen electronics, but if you had the courage to walk through the beaded curtain, the back rooms offered more.

They browsed, finding a hot plate with a corner where the white plastic had been toasted like a marshmallow, a space heater with screws missing, a power strip a dog had gotten at, and a bronze desk lamp with the green glass dome that his father insisted was the exact same kind they had in the University of Chicago library.

"These things are all damaged," he announced, parking the space heater on Mel's glass-top counter. "So I'll expect a serious discount."

Mel's eyes rolled. He drew his good hand from one pocket

and scratched the gnarled stub where his left hand once had been.

"Twenty bucks," said Hartley's father. "For everything. Twenty-five tops."

Mel dragged glazed eyes across the things in Hartley's arms. Cobwebs and dead bug parts clogged the empty socket of the green lamp. "Forty-five."

Hartley's father laughed. "Come on, Mel, I haven't even perused the back rooms yet. You don't want to drive away a customer before he's even finished shopping. I'm thinking of buying my son a sword."

Mel cast a hateful look at Hartley. "Fine," he said. "Twenty-five."

The first room down the back hallway had racks of cracked leather jackets and polyester suits people had died in. The second room peddled lethal exotics, cases full of Nazi bayonets and guns so small they looked like weapons for toddlers. There were throwing stars and tooth necklaces here, a wall of battle-axes. Then, at the end of the hall, a walk-in closet with floor-to-ceiling shelves full of skin magazines heavy with the oil off people's hands.

Hartley's father liked to take his time going through the back—trying on the biker jackets, digging through the buckets full of belt buckles, testing the balance on all the throwing knives in all the glass cases—so Hartley made his way directly to the last room, locating again the one magazine called *Sexpot,* which he knew had a series of naked women riding horses through mountain meadows. Back when Hartley first discovered this issue, he imagined there might actually be a ranch somewhere out west where the models and their horses hung out all day, washing their hair and eating carrots, waiting for the most ideal summer weather to go out and do the next photo shoot. It was a place that had entered his dreams long ago, and he still entertained the naïve fantasy that someday he'd try to find it.

But the pages with the horseback women had been torn out, and all that was left, besides the phone sex ads, was a spread titled "Damsels in Distress!" A blonde on a hospital bed with blood running down her chin and chest; a blonde in a pleated skirt with a jump rope noosed around her neck; a blonde in a hard hat and denim cutoffs with a saw blade embedded in her torso. He leafed through them, each page tearing loose from the ruined binding, until he came to the last picture, of a woman trapped in an overturned car. She looked less fakely pornographic than the others, more plausibly distressed, with her dark hair and judicious green eyes, a sensible yellow blouse. The shirt had been torn open in a revealing way, but the over-all effect—of her ribs stabbing out her torso and the sickening curve of her neck, of the broken auto glass studding one side of her face, the blood welling up across her cheek, the embedded blue diamonds turning into rose quartz, into dark wet rubies—

"*Psst!* Earth to Hartley." A finger flicked his earlobe.

He glanced back at his father.

"Ooh, nice. What is she? A zombie or something? Excellent. Have you seen the new movie about the zombie apocalypse?"

Hartley gathered the loose pages of wrecked women and stowed them on a shelf of water-damaged *Playboys*. "Which movie?"

His father shrugged. "It's our future, I guess. But I haven't actually seen it."

Hartley felt it then, perhaps for the first time, the silent advance of Fate taking a step closer. Something was about to happen, he thought. Good or bad. Something. He knew it.

As his father drove them away, down that derelict city street, Hartley looked out at the world, trying to see what was coming to him. Pawnshops and liquor stores, steel bars on every window. What, he thought, am I not seeing?

Back at the shipping container, his father set the library lamp on the minifridge beside his mattress and said, "Well, I guess I'm nesting." He pulled the brass chain and the steel room filled with soft green light. When all of his new appliances had proven themselves to him he got two beers from the fridge and pulled a pair of tattered beach chairs to the open end of the container so they could watch the orange evening sky fade beyond the shipping canal.

"Just the men tonight. Who needs anybody else."

Hartley nipped at his beer. The stale froth combined with a rotten whiff of the canal made his stomach shudder.

His father finished his first beer and opened a new one. "But what do you suppose she's doing tonight, without us?"

Hartley thought of the girls on the erotic horse ranch. Another night eating carrots, a pillow fight, a kissing closet. But he was already graduating from this fantasy, as there were real girls in school with bodies he might soon get to touch. The old dreams were fading, real life showing through at the edges. The horse ranch wasn't the future anymore. The future was a girl he'd meet on spring break of sophomore year, two singles hedging at the perimeter of a blaring Florida dance floor, stealing away to share a tallboy on a seawall as sand crabs scuttled beneath their dangling feet, two midwesterners sharing stories of having suffered the same long winters, the same luckless summer baseball. The future was a marriage six years later, honeymooning in the islands, room service every night, love on the beach under a new moon. The future was a shift from protected sex, to careful sex, to hopefully procreative sex, to the anxious nightly coupling of people losing faith that any kind of sex could bring them what they really wanted. *Will we,* her eyes sometimes asked, *ever have a child?* The future was a big house in the suburbs, with Glennis trapped inside all day with wine, with gin, washing back the neighbor's pain pills, asleep at the dinner table, wasted at the company picnic, naked in the boss's koi pond, minor interventions, major interventions, drunk behind the wheel, *Are you sure you're okay to drive?*

"What did you just say?" his father barked.

Hartley looked out over the shipping canal. The clouds glowed above the distant skyscrapers like warm coals. He felt far away from himself. "Nothing."

His father glared at him for a time, then opened another beer. "I was asking you," he said, "what your mom's doing tonight."

Hartley turned around and looked into the dark cramped space of the shipping container.

Then the dream begins to fade. Consciousness creeps closer. The beast in the dark breathes to the cadence of a sleeping rapist. The corrugated steel of the freight unit wants to dissolve into the flat concrete of a cell wall. He shuts his eyes again, harder. Chasing after the reverie. Anything to pass these final hours of captivity.

"I think Mom went out for Indian food again," Hartley explained.

"*In*dian food." His father forced breaths through his nose. "I believe *that*. Who eats Indian food?"

"Yeah, she doesn't even like it."

The lights of half a dozen planes hovered in a perfect dotted line connecting down toward Midway. Hartley was sure they were both seeing this, but turning to his father he realized the man's thoughts were somewhere else.

"If she doesn't like it, then why would she eat it?"

Hartley closed one eye and reached out, touching each sparkling blip in the sky.

"If she doesn't even like it," his father repeated, "then what? Someone's making her eat it?"

"Mr. Gupta," said Hartley.

The beer can stopped short of his father's face. "Who's Mr. Gupta?"

Mr. Gupta was the man who taught the entrepreneurs' course Hartley's mother had begun taking on Wednesday nights.

"Entrepreneurs' course?" His father stood up, patting his thighs like he was going to rush off in the car at that very moment. But this was the night the car wouldn't start, the night his father would eventually fall into a deep drunk sleep in that lawn chair, the night Hartley would walk two miles to a gas station in the dark to call his mother for a ride home.

"Mis-ter Gup-ta." His father shaped carefully the name of the man who would, in time, become Hartley's stepfather. "Entrepreneurs' course."

Then came a shift in the wind and Hartley caught the full stench of the canal—the rust and mushy tires, the toxic fish skeletons, the reek of the cell toilet. The green belt of lamplight stretched out in front of them, unfurling all the dim promises of a future they could suddenly see quite well but do nothing about.

I see it now, Hartley thinks, remembering the soft green glow of university life, the charmed career, the big house, the love of this or any life. All of it suddenly dissolving in a rush of fluorescent light and the hollering of prison guards announcing a new day.

THE INTERVENTION SO FAR

A wicked brand of storm had been brewing since dusk, but then the drapes fell still and the stagnant tyranny of August returned without a drop of rain. Emmit Page could smell a sweet rankness he thought might've been the ripening cornfields coming through his living room window, then the phone rang. It was his son-in-law calling to explain that Glennis had taken off all her clothes at a dinner party. It didn't seem like the kind of emergency to be calling about so late at night, but Hartley insisted that this was a nearly unforgivable thing for her to have done. The other guests at the party were important business colleagues, brokers and traders, people like Hartley working in downtown Chicago turning the dials of the midwestern economy.

Hartley, who worked in farm futures at the mercantile exchange, had once tried to explain his job to Emmit by stating that if he could simply predict September's price of corn in August it would make him very rich. Hartley clung to the notion that he and his father-in-law weren't so different, insisting occasionally that Emmit, living as he did in Wicklow, must've known things about the farm end of the business.

"She's drunk, sir," Hartley said. "So drunk this week I don't know what to do."

Emmit muted the volume on the baseball game. "It's difficult to put clothing back on a drunk woman," he said. "Can you get something big, like a sheet or a tarp maybe?"

"We're already home," Hartley explained. "She's asleep in the foyer now. I'm calling to ask if you could come up here and help me confront her." He paused, waiting for Emmit to agree. "I'm thinking," he added, "of staging an intervention."

Emmit moved to the window where the last etchings of daylight were being pinched between a dark bank of clouds on the horizon and the night sky above. He saw his son-in-law infrequently these days, on holidays mostly, fancy dinners at their house in Tower Hill. Less frequently did they come to Wicklow. But the very first time Emmit met his son-in-law had been when they came to announce their plans to marry, or, as Hartley had put it, to ask permission to do so. Emmit couldn't recall much suspense in it—Glennis already had a rather conspicuous engagement ring on her finger—but he ended up liking Hartley for the gesture anyway. And later on, when the two men stepped outside to smoke the cigars Hartley had brought, his future son-in-law promised to give Glennis a big house in the suburbs. Emmit wasn't worried about that, but he didn't know how to tell this young man that he was entering a life in which Emmit himself had once been trapped.

"We had plans for dinner tomorrow night," Hartley went on. "But I've canceled that and arranged this instead. The intervention, I mean. And if you could make it, sir, it would mean a lot to me. To Glennis."

When Emmit finally agreed, his son-in-law's voice became suddenly more upbeat, like a salesman rushing the call to a conclusion before minds could change. "Okay then," Hartley said. "Tomorrow it is." And the line went dead.

Out the window, the distant bank of weather had merged with the darkness and he could no longer tell where the calm gave way to the trouble. Emmit turned back to the TV, where a catcher chased a ball to the backstop while runners stole bases. He dialed his friend.

"You watching this crap?" Rick said. "Fucking Cubs. All this money on the field and still the product sucks."

"My son-in-law just called," said Emmit. "Sounds like Glennis is on a bender. I gotta go see them tomorrow. Mind if I drop by your place tonight?"

Rick's TV announced more chaos while Emmit's muted set showed a ball drifting into the outfield bleachers, visitors jogging home. "Same shit over and over," Rick mumbled.

//

Rick's house sat on a hill overlooking the south end of Wicklow. A sprawling piece of land with a view, in daylight, of the burned-out trailer park that Rick had turned into a post-apocalyptic paintball battlefield. And beyond that, on a clear day, one could see the cemetery where Janice was buried.

"An intervention, huh?" Rick dropped himself into a bank of stuffed leather chairs set up in front of a home theater screen.

"I don't see much point in it," Emmit said. "But Hartley asked, and I haven't got any plans for the weekend. How about you? You wanna come along for this?"

Rick stared at the TV as the pitching coach strode to the mound.

"Glennis always liked you," Emmit said. "I think she used

to have sort of a crush on you. On the uniform, anyway. Did you know she wanted to join the Navy back in high school?"

"They're down nine runs in the eighth," said Rick. "And *now* they're giving the pitcher some advice?"

"Honestly, though," Emmit continued. "The message might sound more convincing coming from a sailor."

Rick leaned forward, his face gathering the forlorn blue light off the television, and Emmit recalled the many times the two of them had tried to help save Janice from herself.

"I'm not sure the messenger matters," Rick said, "when it's an ambush."

//

As he was driving alone back through town, the Lumina's power steering finally gave out. Emmit muscled the car to the side of the road and left it. The walk home took him through Oak Hill Cemetery, squeezing through the fence where he knew there was a loose bar. There wasn't much trash at Janice's grave this time—just a crumpled can of High Life and an empty pack of Marlboros—but someone had spray-painted a reaper's scythe on the back of the headstone, so Emmit took off his blazer and hung it there. A good fit, he thought as he gathered the trash and then stood a moment longer, thinking what to say, listening to the bugs hum in the trees.

After dark, the cemetery always smelled vaguely toxic, but not in such a terrible way. It reminded him of drinking beer in the quarry in high school, he and Janice and Rick, with the waft of the heavy metals oxidizing in the water at the bottom of the basin. A premonition of the rust that would eventually spread over the whole town, but a trigger for nostalgia just the same.

He took a deeper breath and a knot clenched in his throat. He wanted to explain about Glennis, but the lump in his neck swelled and hardened. In the distance, the headlights of a maintenance truck bumped along the far edge of the cemetery grounds. He knelt to the turf, trying to draw a full breath, but the air was too thick with memory, with history. Alarm bells clanged inside his head. Sirens rang out in the night. Then it was quiet again.

//

The next morning, as the Prairie Stater carried him toward the city, Emmit made his way to the lounge car, where there were bigger windows and booths to stretch out in. The corn rushed by as if on a conveyor belt. Despite the assumptions of people like Hartley, Emmit knew nothing about farming. For years he'd traveled the world selling tires, but more recently he spent his days at a sales desk for a company that made foundation sealant. Gold Seal was a metallic yellow liquid that turned gray as it dried. His office had a window that looked out onto a parking lot. Beyond that was a state highway, a Home Depot, and then a green sea of corn to the horizon.

In Chicago, he boarded a commuter service that whisked him north of the city. Forty minutes later he stepped off the platform into Tower Hill at a posh suburban intersection with banks on three of its corners. A light rain fell. Hartley had given walking directions to their house, but before Emmit could get the paper out of his pocket a silver Audi rolled up to the curb with his son-in-law's face in the window.

"She's at the salon right now," Hartley reported as Emmit got into the car. The seat belt had turned up the collar of his raincoat, making him look like someone playing a private eye.

"It's nice to see you again, Hartley."

"Yes, sir," he said. "I'm sorry. It's good to see you too." Hartley pulled through town, listing Glennis's transgressions—*She fell asleep in this park . . . She made quite a scene at that restaurant . . . These people, in the blue house, are no longer our friends*—down a street full of shops selling luggage and imported furniture, until he stopped in front of a frosted window with scissors painted on the glass. "She's in there right now." Hartley glanced at the dashboard clock. "She'll be done any minute. Just watch. She'll stumble out and get in her car. She drives drunk everywhere. We can follow her and you'll see how bad it is."

"I can imagine," Emmit told him. They sat watching the storefront for a time, suburban ladies occasionally emerging, opening umbrellas over their too-new hair. "Is there a place to get a sandwich?" Emmit finally asked. "I haven't eaten all day."

Hartley stared at the salon window for another moment, then drove a few blocks down to a café with French art on the walls and butcher paper tablecloths. When he didn't order anything for himself, Emmit asked for two BLTs.

"Glen's told me about her mom," said Hartley. "She says it was much worse with your wife."

Emmit drank his water, watching his son-in-law's face distort through the bottom of the glass. "I'd bet it's about the same."

Hartley went on about the intervention, describing what he figured it might achieve. Eventually the sandwiches showed up and Hartley stopped talking.

"How are the markets treating you?" Emmit asked.

Hartley pushed his fries around his plate. "It would help

if you could tell me exactly how the September corn looks down your way."

"It's still August corn right now, isn't it?"

A smile flickered at the corners of Hartley's mouth.

"My office looks over a cornfield," Emmit said. "I'll give you a report on Monday."

Hartley eyed the window. "Don't you think this'll take longer than that?"

"A lot longer, I'm sure."

As they drove back across town, Hartley explained that Glennis would be out all afternoon shopping and beautifying for what she expected would be a dinner at the house with a retired anthropology professor she'd had in college, but would really be the intervention, with their minister and Glennis's doctor and a woman from New Horizons Sobriety Clinic. "And us too, of course," Hartley added. "The others will be more like mediators, while you and I state grievances."

As they waited for the garage door to open, Emmit stared at the house. The rain had paused and their new copper gutters blazed absurdly in the afternoon sun. Hartley began a new tour inside the house, again narrating Glennis's troubles—*She spent a whole night on this hardwood . . . She fell down these steps—* until they'd come to the guest room.

"Tonight it ends," the younger man said, chopping the edge of one hand against his open palm. "Before she becomes some kind of tragedy."

//

With Janice, Emmit had intervened occasionally, and occasionally his wife had curbed her drinking, but never for long. It went

like that for years until one day he came home from a sales trip
to find her blacked out on a couch in the basement. Glennis,
then just an infant, he found in the empty bathtub. While the
paramedics took Janice to the hospital, Emmit put his daughter
in his car. The highway made a straight line to the sky and the
fields of corn and soy spread out limitless on both sides. They'd
start over on their own, he'd thought, someplace else. They'd go
to the city, where he had friends. Or to the mountains, where
he knew no one at all.

"That's not who I married," he'd said, turning to the child
in the backseat. "That is someone else entirely."

But the baby wasn't listening. The baby was asleep. And somehow, hours later, they ended up back home again. He still had
years more to put up with, waiting for disaster, inching toward
divorce. It wasn't until Janice turned up in that motel room that
Emmit finally left Wicklow, hiding his daughter from the stares
and whispers for the duration of her school years. But all along
Emmit held on to the old house, until one day, after Glennis left
for college, he packed up the car and drove back home for good.

//

Downstairs, he found the reverend picking deviled eggs off a
cold-food platter. They discussed addiction as the minister led
the way into the library, where Glennis's doctor and the liaison
from the sobriety clinic sat on wingback chairs sipping coffee.
In turn, they each made note of their knowing about Janice.

"What exactly do you know?" Emmit asked.

"That she also struggled with alcohol," the doctor said.

"Oh," said Emmit. "Yes, that's true."

"A double burden," said the liaison in her soft, clinical voice.

"Every family has one," Emmit told them, trying to sound jolly. "I got two."

Hartley rushed into the room. "Someone's pulling into the driveway." He made a quick count of chairs. "Everybody be quiet, and I'll call her in." A minute passed, then another. No doors opened, though a knocking could eventually be heard. Hartley chugged out of the room, returning minutes later with a silver-haired man in a blue blazer, tan slacks breaking over penny loafers. A slender paper bag hung at his side, a bottle of brown liquor peeking out.

"Everyone," Hartley said, his forehead pinching, "this is Professor Vincent Ash."

The professor's attention lingered on the minister before finally returning to Hartley. "I guess I didn't understand what you were asking me to do. Was I only supposed to *pretend* to come over for dinner?"

"That's okay," Hartley said. "The more we have, the stronger we are. Should we go over our roles again?"

"Maybe you should sit down," said the doctor.

Hartley palmed the back of a chair, appearing to agree with the idea before shaking it off. "No, I've got to stay on my feet for this. Can I get anything for anyone? More coffee?" His eyes cased the room, finding each of his guests in turn. "It's funny," he added, putting on a wounded smile. "I could actually *use* a drink right now."

The professor set the bottle of scotch loudly on a glass side table. "An intervention, huh." He glanced around the room. "How's it going so far?"

Then a door opened and shut at the other end of the house. Footsteps across the kitchen floor.

Hartley's back straightened. His eyes widened on Emmit.

He cleared his throat. "Honey . . . ?" he called out into the silence. "Glen, is that you? I'm in the library."

He stopped to listen. Everyone waited. The moment filled and filled with anticipation, as if they were a surprise party hiding in the dark.

"Sweetheart . . . ?" he called again. "Can you . . . can you come in here?"

The footsteps started up again, padding closer, until Rick LaForge appeared in the doorway.

"Oh, Christ," Hartley muttered, pressing out the door without a greeting.

Rick surveyed the room, locating Emmit. He said, "I decided to come after all."

Hartley came back a moment later with a chair for the professor, then he left again to go sit on a padded bench in the foyer with a view of the driveway.

In the library, the sun dropped into the stained-glass window and the waiting became even more awkward with everyone's face cut up into so many colors. Eventually, Hartley came in to get a cup of coffee and stand by himself in the corner, glaring at Rick, who carried on loudly to the clinical experts about his own continuing venture into sobriety. Then the room dimmed as night came on and the conversation meandered into more accessible topics—hapless Chicago baseball and the terrible heat, the way windows stick in such humidity.

"I heard something," Hartley interrupted. "A car door. Did anyone else hear that?" But judging by the glances moving around the room Emmit could tell no one had heard anything.

The reverend was the first to give up, announcing that he had Sunday services in the morning. Then the doctor left, and the woman from New Horizons. Emmit watched them under the driveway floodlight, shaking their heads. Then it began to rain again and they rushed into their cars and sped off.

"I can't say I'm entirely shocked we lost this little showdown," the professor said, strolling toward the door in the manner of someone accustomed to taking leave with ceremony. "Your wife wasn't much of an anthropology student. The study of human progress requires a bit less cynicism, I think, and better attendance too. But somehow she got an *A* anyway." He smiled and clapped Hartley on the shoulder. "Glennis has remarkable resolve."

When the old man finally let himself leave, Emmit brought the cold platter to the kitchen table, where he pulled out a chair for Hartley. They ate spinach dip and cheese and crackers.

"She has remarkable resolve," Hartley said in a mocking voice.

The powder room door opened and Rick came into the kitchen still buckling his pants. Hartley's face curdled.

"Resolve, sure," Rick agreed, scraping a chair backward and joining them at the table. "It's the rest of us who are weak with sobriety."

"Is that what AA teaches you?" Emmit asked.

"More or less."

"I wouldn't say I feel 'weak,'" Hartley said.

Rick scooped up a handful of crackers. "I'm just saying I've been where Glennis is now. I've been the one lying in the gutter while all my friends were waiting to help."

"She's not exactly in 'the gutter,'" Hartley said. "She's probably at a wine bar right now. The place serves sushi."

"Every gutter's different." Rick reclined, tossing a cracker into his mouth. "But it's still a gutter."

"Anyway," said Emmit, "I think the point is that this process may take some time."

Rick yawned, looking around. "How many bedrooms does this place have?"

Hartley only stared back at the question, then rose and retrieved the bottle of scotch the professor had brought. He poured two drinks, then said, his voice taking a sharp formality, "I assume, Rick, that you won't be partaking."

Rick only grinned at the amber glasses, and said, "Think it's time I hit the sack."

When they were alone again, Hartley loosened. He sighed and said, "Glennis was always a bit wild, but I liked that about her. You know, like in college. But now, I don't know, I want to have kids. I don't know if we *can* have kids, but even if we could, how would that work?" He put a piece of cheese between crackers, looking to Emmit, as he held the tiny sandwich between finger and thumb, like a sad giant.

"The booze I felt I could handle," Hartley continued. "Lots of booze, sure. But then there were painkillers. I swear everyone around here has a prescription for something. And then, last month, her girlfriend came into town, her old roommate, Denise, you remember her. She came in for the weekend, Denise did, and they ended up snorting *heroin* together." Hartley put the little sandwich in his mouth and crunched it up. "Look at where I live," he said, flicking a crystal bowl at the center of the table, glancing up into the skylights. "Do you think anyone around here does *heroin*?"

For dessert they cut the big chocolate-dipped strawberry in half, and this seemed to signify their giving up as well. So they refilled their glasses of scotch and sat down in front of the baseball game. And later, when they got tired of getting up for more ice, they just poured lukewarm scotch straight from the bottle.

"Neat," said Emmit, lifting a sarcastic toast.

Hartley tipped his glass back, downing half of it in a single gulp, making a face. It reminded Emmit of the way teenagers drink, suffering the flavor in order to impress friends, to impress girls, to just get high. But his son-in-law didn't care for the high any more than he did for the flavor of the oak barrel. When Hartley was finally able to shed the sour face, he topped himself off again, saying, "I don't get it, what's so *neat* about it?"

Emmit couldn't say. And he couldn't tell if Hartley was punning or not. He felt drunk. The baseball game played on two TVs that merged whenever he blinked. He topped off his own drink, gulping toward his own deepening high, each sip a communion with Glennis's addiction.

Later, when the bottle got low, a voice said, *It's about time they got him out of there,* and Emmit looked up to see the starting pitcher getting pulled. At this, Hartley levered himself off the couch, setting his empty glass loudly onto the coffee table, excusing himself to the bathroom.

Later still, Emmit snapped awake again to a heavy metallic groaning. He looked around for Hartley, who'd never returned from the bathroom. The glassware rattled in the kitchen cabinets. An earthquake, he thought. Then the groaning abruptly ceased. Just the garage door grinding open, he realized. He sat up, then stood, drunk fingers fumbling to re-button the top of his shirt. He tried to shake off the panic that was twisting upward from his chest, hardening like a tumor in his throat, as if he were a teenager again with parents coming home early to catch him drinking. He waited, swaying in place, blinking, his vision doubling and undoubling, but the angry parent didn't appear. Glennis didn't appear. It was

Glennis he was waiting for. *I'm* the parent, he thought. I'm the one in control.

When she still didn't appear, Emmit walked out through the mudroom into the empty two-car garage, breathing for a moment the fumes left behind by Hartley's car. The big door was still open behind where the silver Audi had been parked, and he walked out into the drizzling evening, into a silence that wasn't so different from the one that washed nightly over Wicklow. A sound of air conditioners dutifully toiling, of single cars shushing down sleepy roads. Maybe Hartley was leaving her, he thought. For good, he hoped. But then a siren came whining through the quiet suburban night and its tensing pitch brought the panic back into Emmit's throat. Another siren from a different direction. Then another. The deep braying of a fire truck.

//

Hours later, rowing through dreams, Emmit woke on the couch to Glennis softening her hand against the stubble of his cheek. As she leaned over, her long straight hair fell toward him, making a dim tunnel around her face, her big dark pupils pink around the edges, the eyelids slumping low, her blouse hanging inelegantly from her frame. And for a moment, Emmit felt relieved. This is not my daughter, he thought. This is someone else.

"We've been waiting for you," he told her, trying to sit up. He looked around for Hartley, as if it were time now to begin stating grievances. But the evidence in every direction—the raided cold platter, the half-empty bottle of scotch—scuttled the idea that they'd ever been trying to help anyone.

His daughter laid a hand on Emmit's chest, pressing him down, dragging a quilt off the arm of the couch and covering him with it. Then she was gone again, and he could only hear the tick-ticking of her fingers killing the house's lamps.

//

At dawn, he walked upstairs and shook Rick awake in the guest bed. They packed their things quietly, got in Rick's truck, and headed home. Emmit moved back into his house, unplugging all the phones and opening all the windows, stripping the beds, throwing the sheets into a pile on the laundry room floor. He got the Lumina towed to a service station, paid his bills, ate dinner in front of the ballgame.

The night after passed slowly, a montage of strange and dispiriting dreams of stained-glass faces and howling sirens, of a long-dead woman looking down on him from above.

At work on Monday, he stared at his computer, at his phone, out the window. The sky turned yellow. There were birds everywhere and then no birds. Rain and then hail. A piece of ductwork lifted off the Home Depot and rose up into the clouds. Everyone in the office rushed down to the basement, but Emmit stayed behind and listened to the sound a window makes when it curves.

When the storm passed, he was the first person in the whole county to walk out into the ensuing calm. Everything wet shone in the sun like a kind of gold that wouldn't last. He crossed the parking lot and the state highway, found himself a quarter mile into that field of corn—September's crop in August. He put his hands in the dirt, on the stalks, pulled down one particular ear, shucked it, and let the breeze carry away the silk. He tried to discern how the crop was faring, tried to imagine whether prices might rise or fall. He put his ear to it, listening. The naked corn felt like that hand on his cheek, waking him again into the truth that people with so little control of their own lives have so much power over ours.

ARE YOU A FRIEND

"These beetles are making my life miserable," Mona said. "People look at a house and they like it, they want to buy it, but then they say, 'But how will it look without any trees?' And then I say, in my politest voice, 'These aren't *all* oak trees, this is Tower Hill, everything's fine here, there's no need for alarm.' But of course it's the middle of winter and everything looks dead." Mona glanced around the Lowerys' living room, so elegant but dark. With a little staging—a bit more light, a bit less clutter— she could sell their house in a minute. "People just aren't very bright anymore," she continued. "The younger buyers especially. Like what's-her-name, Leonard's new girlfriend. She's young, but I've heard she's quite dim too. A *loose* sort of girl. I don't know, I hate to say it, I really do, but is *slut* too strong a word?"

Vera Lowery stared off into the corner of the room. "I'm sorry," she said, turning to Mona. "Did you say something?"

"I was just talking about Leonard. I know he isn't my husband anymore, but— Oh, never mind." Mona gave up. There was still only one topic of conversation on these visits. She glanced out the window to where the Lowerys' handyman was sweeping snow off the walkway between the garage and the house. "So," Mona sighed, restarting, "I heard Hartley Nolan just got sentenced. Eight years doesn't seem like nearly enough." She watched Vera closely, trying to gauge whether this was the first time she was hearing this news. But Vera's attention slid off into the corner of the room where her deceased daughter's face stared back from an easel plastered with photos.

Mona looked at the easel too, which had been put together months ago for the funeral, along with several others like it, each one documenting an era of Sonia's life. They'd been brought home from the funeral parlor and left like traps all over the house, waiting around corners, in half-darkened rooms, Sonia's piercing green eyes ambushing you on the way to the bathroom. Somebody rearranged them every few days. The handyman, probably, though what else he did anymore wasn't clear to Mona. There were baskets of rotten sympathy flowers still in some rooms, a pile of melted candles and ice-crusted teddy bears at the base of the sickly oak out front.

"But what I really think we should discuss," Mona said, "is getting this house listed as soon as possible. Come spring, the market will heat up fast."

Vera's husband materialized in the doorway, pale and hunched. You couldn't take a step on this old-growth flooring without announcing yourself, but Bart Lowery, as he shuffled across the room, made no sound at all. Lame for decades since falling off a chairlift in Jackson Hole, his body had been failing more rapidly of late—spinal fusions, nerve damage, incontinence even—and now the crushing loss of a child.

"You two need a new beginning." Mona looked out the window again, at the handyman now in the driveway. He was glaring at her BMW. "I'll stage the heck out of this house for you," Mona said. "I'll trim the dead branches off that oak. I'll fix that railing out front—"

"Oh, I'll have Raymond take care of the railing," Vera interjected.

Bart Lowery made a sound in his nose, but when Mona turned to him his eyes had closed. "Yes, well that actually leads me to another thought," Mona said. "That garage apartment should be empty for the sake of selling the property."

Vera's back straightened. "Oh dear, Raymond will *not* take kindly to that idea."

Bart's eyes opened, a smile tugging his lips. "Especially if he hears it came from you, Mona."

Mona offered an acquiescent little frown, her dislike of Raymond Bello being no secret. That the Lowerys kept a handyman on full-time wasn't so outlandish, she supposed— the need was there, and they could certainly afford it—but Mona had never understood how they'd let him settle into an uncle's role. A grown man without a family of his own, with his mumbled greetings and his spattered clothes, his everwringing hands. Always present at birthdays and holidays, even driving the children to school.

Once, years ago, Mona came over to pick up her own daughter, who'd been a friend of Sonia's, to find that Vera had gone off to a tennis game and left the handyman in charge. The handyman! Mona said some harsh words to Vera over the phone that evening, then some harsher words in person days later in the Lowerys' driveway, which Raymond Bello had undoubtedly heard through his open windows—that she found him to be grimy and strange and unfit, and that if Vera and Bart were going to abdicate their roles as parents, they might hire a nanny instead.

Always, with Mona, a rift of one kind or another eventually developed. It was what her ex-husband once described as her "expiration date." Inevitably, people grew weary or offended. Neighbors raised a fence. Friends stopped calling. But then, just days after their spat, Vera showed up at Mona's door for their regular Tuesday coffee as though nothing had happened.

It turned out to be the handyman who held the grudge, with his hateful glances and his terse replies. But in the end, he wasn't Mona's concern. After all, what kind of man dispatched himself to a life of tinkering with kitchen appliances? To living alone above someone else's garage? And even when the tools went missing from Mona's garden shed a week later, she felt sure that this was the worst such a person could do.

The back door whined open and boot steps could be heard coming through the house. The unpuckering of the seal on the fridge door. Then the handyman appeared in the living room doorway with a flap of cheese in his hand.

"Raymond," Bart said, "Mona thinks you ought to be fixing that railing."

The old man's forehead creased, small eyes blinking behind his wire glasses.

Vera frowned at her husband. "We were just *talking* about the railing is all. We're just talking about the house in general."

Bello turned to Vera to estimate the breadth of this gathering betrayal. "The house, ma'am?"

"About *selling* the house," Mona interjected. "The Lowerys have decided to move."

The handyman's brow collapsed and he cast a long despairing gaze into the blackened maw of the fireplace. It was the same look he'd worn months earlier when he'd learned of Sonia's death. On the morning following the accident, Mona had come to the house to offer support, but Vera and Bart were still out tending to the earliest business of the tragedy. After trying the front door, she came around back to wait until the Lowerys returned. For several minutes she stood in the drizzle, patiently facing the house as though she were still expecting someone to let her inside, when a throat clearing startled her from behind.

"Raymond," she'd said, turning, "you scared me."

Bello rubbed his hands on a rag.

"I've brought something." Mona shook the paper bag. "I had to bring *some*thing."

"Okay." He shrugged, extending a greasy hand. "I sign for deliveries all the time."

"I'm not the UPS man, Raymond." Mona glanced down the driveway. "It's just bagels is all. But what are you supposed to bring on a day like this?"

He yawned, squinting at a mess the squirrels had made of the bird feeder.

"Oh my God," she said, "you don't know what's happened, do you?" She watched him try to put it together—the wailing sirens in the night, the predawn car backing down the driveway.

It was the same look on his face now in the Lowerys' living room, hearing again such awful news from the woman who thought him "strange" and "unfit." He stood speechless as the conversation moved on without him, as Mona explained how she planned to stage the Lowerys' house.

"I have a storage unit full of antiques that'll fit perfectly here. Lamps especially, to brighten things." When she looked at Bello again, the cheese was wadded in his fist, threads of yellow mush worming out between his fingers. He turned and trudged off, reappearing in the same window as before, stomping toward his apartment over the garage.

Bart made an unimpressed sound. "How many years has he been living up there, rent free? And now he's going to throw a fit?"

"For some people it's never enough," Mona agreed.

Vera nodded absently, gazing again at the easel in the corner. "Yes," she muttered. "Eight years isn't nearly enough."

//

Mona had met the killer once, years earlier. He and his wife had been looking at houses around Tower Hill, and when Mona's partner was on vacation, she took the young couple herself to view a ranch-style near the post office. Hartley Nolan wore dark blue jeans and dock shoes, a merino sweater. The wife had a wry smile and a sensual voice and had come to the showing wearing aviator sunglasses and a hooded college sweatshirt. Not the type of girl Mona might've expected to be with a stock trader, but they were cute together anyway. By the end of the afternoon, she decided they'd end up somewhere better suited to people under forty without any children yet—a condo in the West Loop or a bungalow in Evanston—but a month later they made an offer on a handsome three-bedroom on Cherry Street.

Walking up to this Georgian Colonial now, Mona noticed mail piled on the stoop, soggy newspapers, a smattering of eggshells stuck to the welcome mat.

"Is Glennis in?" she asked a man who opened the door.

"She is not," the man said in an Indian accent. Sweat stains bloomed in the armpits of his button-down. A gnarled wad of packing tape clung to the thigh of his slacks. Behind him, boxes were stacked in the foyer. He asked in a doubtful voice, "Are you a friend?"

"My agency helped the Nolans find this house," Mona explained. "And now we're going to help them sell it." She passed him her business card. "*Are* they selling it?"

The man introduced himself as Hartley Nolan's stepfather. As he spoke, he cast a wary look onto the street behind her. From somewhere deeper inside the house a woman's voice conducted a phone conversation. "*. . . I haven't seen her since the sentencing . . . yes . . . or that's my assumption, on some kind of bender . . .*"

"Glennis is . . . out," the stepfather said, his eyes continuing to worry over the street. "Is that man with you?"

Mona turned around. At the curb, watching them from the passenger seat of her BMW, was Raymond Bello.

Mona shook the stepfather's hand and rushed back across the frozen lawn. The passenger window was down, and the handyman, as he watched her approach, bore the determined look of a rodent.

"You don't know me at all," Bello began. "I was a harbor welder . . . I know how to keep things safe—"

"What the hell are you talking about, Raymond?"

"I'm talking . . ." he said. "Mr. and Mrs. Lowery . . . they need . . . I can help . . ." He seemed to have a compelling speech going inside his head, only a fraction of which was actually reaching the surface. Mona had never heard the man string more than two full sentences together, and as he spoke now his words came in spits and chokes.

"Get out of my car," she said, striding around to the driver's seat.

He climbed out onto the curb, glaring hatefully at the Nolans' house before turning and putting his withered hands on the open sill of the car door. "You don't understand," he said, craning into the car. He tried to smile now, to soften his appearance, but there was a gap in his mouth where a tooth had gone missing and his bloodshot eyes were magnified behind his glasses. "I am like family to them."

It was possible, Mona thought, that he wasn't only trying to preserve his comfortable existence in that garage apartment, that he actually wanted to do right by his grief-stricken landlords. But as Mona looked at the rumpled little peasant begging at the window of her sedan, his turpentine stink lingering inside her car, she couldn't conjure the mercy he'd come for. She glanced past him to make sure the stepfather had gone back into the house, and said, "You can't see it, can you, Raymond?"

"See what?"

"The Lowerys don't actually care about you." She turned the key and the BMW growled to life. "They're just too weak to do this themselves."

//

If the divorce had taught her anything, it was that when other people lose control it's time to seize it for yourself. Late in the divorce proceedings, her husband came to the house one night and threw a fit on the lawn, screaming loud enough for the neighbors to hear. He'd even picked up a dead branch and threatened to smash the mailbox, before growing suddenly exhausted and slinking back to his girlfriend's apartment. This had always been Leonard's complaint, how "exhausting" Mona could be. Even their daughter, grown and married now, living in Colorado, couldn't seem to handle her mother's energy and ambition, her short-fused honesty.

All around her, people lacked the strength and fortitude for real action. It came as some surprise, then, when Mona emerged from her office the next day to find that someone had keyed her BMW. Not a simple scratch but several long deep gouges running parallel across all four panels on the driver's side. And there was also something on the windshield, a bird dropping she thought at first, wadded on one of the wipers, which, upon closer inspection, turned out to be a gob of human phlegm.

She never told Vera and Bart that Raymond Bello had probably stolen her garden tools those years ago. It was the kind of thing she imagined they wouldn't have wanted to hear, or that they *couldn't* have heard. And as she sat inside her BMW while the carwash's high-powered sprayers blasted his phlegm from her windshield, she endeavored to continue insulating her grief-sick friends from details that might unnecessarily complicate their already fragile states. This had been her role always, and especially of late, to pass along the most straight-forward facts pertaining to Sonia's death—Mr. Nolan's name, his blood-alcohol level, the length of his incarceration—but to filter out the community's muddy conjecture.

//

Later that afternoon, as she came to the top of the Lowerys' garage steps, the door opened before she could knock. She thrust a stack of papers into Bello's hands, a dozen listings on the north side of Chicago, and a few, at the very bottom of the pile, of apartments closer to Tower Hill above ethnic restaurants and dog groomers. She tried to move inside, but he held firm in the doorway.

"You don't like me," he said slowly, as if reading from a script. "Fine. But don't do this to *them*."

Leonard had come to flail in this same way. One night drunkenly shouting on the lawn, and the next so polite and sober, quietly insisting that ruining him in the divorce might distress their grown and married daughter. *Don't do this to Liz!* Grown men reducing themselves to helpless, whining children.

She supposed Bart Lowery wasn't any different either, another man losing touch with reality and family at once. As a young father he'd been sweet with his daughters, attentive at least. But as Allie and Sonia grew, he seemed to shirk his connection to them, as if they were just a pair of boarders at the other end of the upstairs hallway. Mona recalled a time when there'd been rumors about a youth minister at the Community Church, something involving an inappropriate relationship with a girl at a previous parish. Child endangerment, people were calling it. Vera had been sick with the news, every day in Mona's kitchen lamenting how Sonia had already been around this minister for months—Sunday school, youth groups, an overnight retreat to a lake in Wisconsin. Yet Vera never actually managed to broach the subject with her daughter. And when Mona finally brought the rumors to Bart's attention, he absorbed the information as if he'd been told his daughter wanted a new pet. "Well," he'd said, "she hasn't mentioned anything like that to *me*."

Her sense of the Lowerys had long been colored by this episode of reckless inertia. Such a charming and attractive bunch, but doomed from the beginning to wear a stain. It was why Mona needed to intervene now—sell the house quick; whisk the grieving parents to a condo; deliver a lasagna to Allie's family. But first, evict the aged freeloader.

"It's already done," she informed the handyman. "If you're not out by Friday, I'm calling the police and telling them you're trespassing. And that you're stealing things."

Bello wheeled around to regard one of the funeral easels, propped up at the foot of his bed. Soccer pictures and Halloween costumes, a school portrait with Sonia missing two teeth.

Mona pressed into the apartment now, its galley kitchen full of dirty dishes, greasy tools all around, a motor laid out on newsprint. An old TV on a milk crate showed a man in a ski mask snipping wires beneath a dashboard. She felt like a parole officer making a surprise visit. "Why does it smell like turpentine in here?" she asked.

At the window, she brushed the curtain aside to see the back of the Lowerys' house, a view into an upstairs bedroom—pink comforter, stuffed animals, shelves of orderly knickknacks—a child's room frozen in time. For a moment, Mona lamented having turned her own daughter's room into a guest suite. Perhaps that's why Liz kept herself in Colorado with her ski bum husband. Then she thought of Sonia's husband, the chemist who became a gravedigger. A vaguely feral sort, but educated, like a scientist who'd turned himself into a werewolf. What had Sonia seen in such a man? Maybe the youth minister *had* fornicated with her.

Liz had long insisted the rumors were true. And Sonia had always shouldered a certain reputation, a shadowy appeal, a looseness. Dark hair in a family of sandy blonds, watchful green eyes, an offbeat dress style suggesting the possibility the Lowerys were hosting an exchange student. A girl whose exotic sensibilities might have insisted on a certain amount of speculation, but not some dumb *slut*!

"What?" The handyman looked out the window, then back at Mona. "Who are you talking to?"

Mona blinked, trying to reorient herself in the present. The smell of turpentine was making her dizzy, nauseous with memory. She glanced around Bello's junky little home, not unlike the old apartment above her father's body shop in the city, with parole officers stopping by now and again to ask their questions. *Tell me, kid, does your father drink a lot? Does he ever do drugs? Where's your mother?* Slowly she regathered her wits, regathered the decades since. She thought: You live in Tower Hill now, Mona. Everything is fine here. No need for alarm. Then she looked at the old con in front of her and smiled.

"What?" he said. "What's so funny?"

"You are, Raymond. You're an absolute joke. I can't have those poor people worrying over some crooked old sponge."

Bello yanked the drapes shut. "If you don't stop this," he said, "I'll . . ." His pink eyes shook in their sockets, then jumped away.

"You'll *what*, Raymond?"

His gaze settled along the far wall. A leather tool belt full of screwdrivers and claw hammers hung from a hook behind the easel.

"Tell me," she said. "What is it exactly that you'll do?"

//

The coming days passed in preparations. A meeting with the appraiser, a man to fix the railing, another to finish wallpapering the dining room. On Sunday, she drove to her storage unit where she kept all the furniture her ex-husband had inherited from his mother. A cache of antique lamps, end tables, and Oriental rugs Mona had won in the divorce, a late-stage windfall after Leonard threw his public fit on the lawn. These were items she didn't actually want to live with but which dressed up the houses she intended to sell. But when she got to the storage facility and raised the big door, her unit was completely empty.

At the front desk, the clerk shrugged. "Sorry," he said. "The cameras in that area haven't been functioning all week."

"But did you see an old man skulking around?" Mona asked. "With wire-rim glasses? Always wringing his hands?"

"Ringing what now?"

"It would have been in the last day or two," she said. "This man has been trying to threaten me recently."

The clerk motioned to the bank of screens on his desk, half of which played static. He leafed through a ring-bound log. "No one's mentioned anything to me," he said, "but if you think a crime has been committed, it's best to call the police."

/

As she drove toward the Lowerys', Mona wondered whether she'd underestimated him. If he'd keyed her car and stolen her staging furniture, was it not also possible that Raymond Bello had snipped her brakes? She felt suddenly afraid that if she didn't slow down heading into the light she too might be killed at a sleepy suburban intersection.

There was a rumor going around that Sonia had been complicit somehow—traveling too fast on that wet street or talking on her phone—in some kind of hurry, people made it sound, to get herself killed. And maybe she *had* been culpable. Maybe she'd seduced the minister to begin with. Maybe the cordial young trader wasn't so much to blame. Mona pressed the brake cautiously, wondering what people would say if Bello *had* sabotaged her car.

Yes, they'd say, *but was she not also complicit in her own death?*

But then the light turned green and her thinking changed, and she turned, no longer bound for the Lowerys', but headed south into the trendy half-urban town that bordered the city.

Leonard answered the apartment door in stretch pants and a neon hoodie.

"Are you running a five-K or something?" she asked.

"Mona," he said, already exhausted, "you can't just show up here."

She pressed into the girlfriend's apartment, down the dim hallway full of movie posters to where a pair of Leonard's mother's lamps bookended a yellow leather couch. "Okay, phew." She scanned the room, noting also some familiar end tables, and the padded Victorian bench.

Leonard stalked onto the red Persian rug. "These were *my* mother's things, Mona, and you weren't even using them—"

"It's okay," she said.

"This stuff," he continued, "it's got sentimental value, to me."

"I said it's okay, Leonard. I'm just relieved that—I don't know—I thought this crazed man was . . ." She swiveled to take in the whole ridiculous apartment, Leonard's mother's antiques mixed with the girlfriend's kitschy Hollywood memorabilia, until she found the girlfriend herself, clad in her own sporty outfit, staring back across the breakfast bar.

"Hi, Mona," the girl said, not unkindly. "Sorry about the B and E we pulled on your storage unit."

"That's okay, Tess. I'm actually relieved it was you guys." It surprised Mona to hear herself forgiving them so quickly, but they looked so stupidly disarming in their Day-Glo jog wear. Plus, she felt disoriented again, as if she *had* crashed at that intersection, then stumbled over here like some dazed amnesiac. And for a long moment she did seem to have lost her memory, just a woman consuming the present without all its ugly contexts. Are these my friends, she wondered. Could this sweet-looking young woman be my daughter? And who is this sporting fellow with the salt-and-pepper goatee? She felt her ribs for damage, her forehead, her teeth. Then her history came reeling back—the long motherless childhood before these years of privilege, marriage, parenthood, divorce. She looked sadly upon her ex-husband. If only, she thought, he hadn't called me a "stupid slut" for all the neighbors to hear.

"Do you need something?" Leonard asked.

Mona put herself down on the leather couch. "I'm feeling poor."

Leonard scoffed. "Poor? Well we both know that isn't true."

"Leonard," said the girlfriend.

Mona slumped back into the couch's deep fleshy clutch. "I mean that I'm feeling a little endangered, I guess."

"En*dang*ered," Leonard repeated.

"I've been at the Lowerys' house all week, helping them through this nightmare, and there's this awful man there who's trying to sabotage me."

Tess set a water glass in front of Mona and sat down beside her. "Which man?"

"Oh God," said Leonard, "not the handyman again." He turned to Tess. "Mona's been warring with this guy for years."

"Oh," said Tess. "You mean Mr. Bello?"

Mona, as she sipped, turned to the girl. Water fell down her chin onto her blouse.

"When I was little," Tess explained, "Sonia Lowery was my babysitter."

Mona wiped her mouth. She felt speechless. How, she wondered, had she not known her ex-husband was shacked up with a girl who'd grown up in Tower Hill? "Why in the world," Mona said, hearing her voice balloon with astonishment, "would Sonia tell you about her parents' handyman?"

"I used to beg her to tell me all sorts of things," Tess answered. "Like ghost stories and stuff. And the creepiest story of all was about a creature from the lake that crawled out of the water at night and put on a suit of human flesh and broke into kids' rooms to steal their tooth fairy money." Tess paused, her eyes lifting ponderously toward the ceiling. "Or maybe it was the teeth he wanted. I can't remember. But the creature's name was definitely *Raymond Bello*." Tess pronounced the name with a disquieting emphasis, as Sonia must once have done. "It was just a story," she continued, "but imagine being a little kid hearing this tale over and over, and then one time, when Sonia's mom was supposed to come pick her up at the end of the night, this random man who wasn't her dad came to the door instead, and she called *him* Mr. Bello." Tess snapped out of her recollective trance and came shrugging back into the present. "It's just so sad. I don't believe in the death penalty, but I hope they hang that guy."

"He got eight years," Mona said.

Leonard made a face. "Not exactly capital punishment."

There were more details to add, Mona thought, about the time she met the killer herself or about the lawyers' attempts to make Sonia complicit, about Hartley Nolan's fancy college degree and Sonia's penchant for wayward ministers. But these people weren't part of Tower Hill's grapevine anymore. They weren't entitled to it.

"I heard he's a terrible alcoholic," Leonard said.

Tess popped off the couch. "No, wasn't it the wife who had the problem?"

"Maybe that's it," Leonard agreed. "Yeah. So, it's actually ironic then."

If Mona had wanted to tell them anything, she'd have told them that the Nolans actually seemed like good people. *I once showed them a house they hated,* Mona could have said, *and they were perfectly nice about it.*

But when she looked up, Leonard was performing a deep knee bend and the girl had propped a leg on the arm of the couch. It was apparently time to run. A siren blared from some unknown distance. The perils of the city loomed close. Dangerous people were everywhere.

Mona laid her hand on one of the stolen end tables. "Is it too late," she murmured, "to call the police?"

//

And then she was in her car, sliding through a rough neighborhood, graffitied and loitered upon, criminals on every corner. The brakes were on the verge of failing, she was sure. She felt dizzy and endangered. Her car still smelled of turpentine. She lifted her phone to her ear. "Liz," she said, "did you know about this nonsense with your father?"

"Which nonsense?"

"The girl he's shacked up with. What do you mean 'which nonsense'? She's younger than you are!"

"Tess is harmless," Liz said. "At least she's getting him back into shape."

Mona thought of the creature Raymond Bello, suited in human flesh, hoarding children's teeth. She thought of his phlegm on her windshield, a wad of shining alien ectoplasm, and of his claws raking the panels of her car. "It's disgusting," said Mona. "Poor Sonia. Do you realize people have tried to make her complicit in all this?"

"Complicit in all what?" her daughter asked.

"And the man who hit her. You should've met him, Liz. He's actually quite decent. He's the type of man I wish you had found—"

"Oh, Jesus. Seriously? Mom, you sound totally out of it right now. Are you okay? Do you need me to call someone?"

"The police maybe. But first I'm going to try to evict him myself."

"Evict who? I don't understand. Is Dad trying to move back in?"

"Did you know this story?" Mona asked. "About the handyman?"

"Which handyman?"

"Please stop being coy with me, Liz. You used to play over there with Sonia. Did she ever say anything about stolen teeth?"

"Mom, seriously, you're not making any sense right now."

"Would you have even told me if there was something to tell?"

"I do think I'm going to call someone, Mom."

"They're too blind to see the trouble he is. It's up to me to cast him out." Mona looked up at the road, surprised to find herself still on it. A red light waited in the distance. She took her foot off the accelerator.

"Mom . . . ?"

The traffic light. It was time to stop. Mona pressed the brake. It felt loose. It didn't feel loose at all.

CAUGHT IN THE CHEMISTRY

He was about to speak, Allie could tell. He was about to make one of his suggestions, which she would then ignore. She was already ignoring it, whatever he was about to say. Andrew's expression said enough—his worried brow, his slowly opening mouth.

He'd been following her around the house all morning, helping locate her phone and purse, handing her the keys to the Range Rover. He'd listened to Allie announce that she was really going this time, in the car, because what was so hard about driving to the grocery store and back? Then Allie went into the garage and sat in her car. She put the keys in the ignition, adjusted the seat, the mirrors. She could feel her husband eavesdropping from the mudroom, his lean shadow on the open door. She adjusted her seat again, looked for her sunglasses. Where the hell were her sunglasses? So she got out again and went back into the house and sat down on the couch to read a magazine instead.

Andrew hadn't been in the mudroom after all. His shadow had been the coat rack. He'd been upstairs getting dressed, but now he was coming back down the steps with his anxious brow, his slowly opening mouth.

"I can tell you're struggling with this first anniversary," he said in the quiet, halting voice he now always used when making suggestions. "Forget about the store. It's time for you to visit the grave."

The Grave, Allie thought, with capital letters. This was how people rendered the memory of her sister. The Grave. The Day. The Spot. A series of vaguely ominous phrases they used—everybody used—to talk around the details of Sonia's death.

"You could even visit Victor while you're down there," Andrew added.

"*Visit* him?" she asked. "Victor didn't like visitors when Sonia was *alive*."

Her husband pressed forward into a lunge. He'd developed a habit of performing light calisthenics during their conversations. "It might actually make you feel better," he said. "Both of you." Everything that came out of Andrew's mouth lately was an invitation to feel better, to better oneself, to self-help. *What about seeing a psychiatrist,* he'd ask. *How about reading a book about the steps to recovery? What about meditation? Let's shake things up with a raw diet! You could start running again. Yeah, running is what you need. Don't you miss running? You should go for a run!* But it was only Andrew who took these suggestions, with his charity races and his weekend yoga, his self-improvement manuals cluttering the house.

"I'm the one who lost a sister, Andrew. Why can't you support me in a more conventional way? Like other men?"

He looked startled by this. "What does *that* mean?"

She wasn't certain what it meant. But her husband was standing in the living room in capri pants drinking a kale shake, looking healthy and organized to such an alarming degree that Allie was beginning to view it as an act of aggression. What had happened to the man who'd once hollowed out the center of a Slim Jim with a power drill in order to make a straw with which to sip his beer? "It means," she said, "that *my* loss is looking an awful lot like *your* midlife crisis."

This of course wasn't fair. And perhaps, she thought, Andrew wasn't entirely wrong. Allie could barely recall the funeral, the burial not at all, sick as she'd been with shock and guilt. Most of what she knew of those events had been relayed to her in secondhand reports—the nice eulogy she'd apparently given, the overwhelming turnout of old friends despite the long drive to Wicklow, the questionable decision by her parents to go with an open casket. The only true memory she possessed was of the moment during the wake, while looking down upon her sister's body, when she realized someone had stolen the wedding ring off Sonia's finger.

It was possible, she began to admit, that her grief was stagnating because she couldn't envision the concrete signifiers of Sonia's death—the plot and the headstone, the cemetery that Victor happened to own. And so, later that morning, when Andrew was in the shower, she left a note on the table that read, *Sorry. You're right about this. I'm walking to the train station now. Tell the kids I'll be back tonight.*

//

She stood on the Metra platform trying to imagine what it must be like to throw oneself in front of a train. Just a month ago, another person had done himself in one station to the south. He was someone Andrew knew, a friend of a friend whom Allie recalled driving his Ferrari convertible in the Fourth of July parade with a bunch of Cub Scouts hanging off the sides.

In downtown Chicago, she got a big sugared pretzel in the station, took two bites, and gave it to a homeless man. Then she boarded the Prairie Stater, choosing a car with a group of young Amish men. Always there were Amish on trains, even when Amish country was nowhere close. It had something to do with technology. A refusal of some kind. At some point in these young men's day they would ride in something horse-drawn. They would churn something. Allie could understand it, the need to refuse. She hadn't driven a car since Sonia's death. She'd tried to get over it, but every time she got behind the wheel of her Range Rover she felt herself turning grim with fate, a precursor to some awful roadside mess.

"Are you Amish?" she asked the young man who sat down beside her.

"*Man*-onite, actually," he said, a lascivious smile cracking through his face. "All man. All night."

Allie turned around. In the seat behind, another young man in a hooded sweatshirt was filming her with a small camcorder. "We're punking you," he explained.

"Is it working?" she asked. She turned to the boy in the seat beside her, his long bushy sideburn coming unstuck from his jaw. "Do *you* feel anything? Because I don't feel a thing."

The boys got up and went to the back of the train car to rethink their strategy.

Allie opened her purse for a mint, discovering a slender paperback that Andrew had left inside titled *So You're Grieving,*

Now What? But it was the memory of her sister that kept Allie from reading any of Andrew's manuals. Sonia had been too self-possessed for such bluntly prescriptive help. The younger sister, yet someone to look up to. Exotically beautiful with dark hair and green eyes, but bored by most boys' attention. Declining invitations to homecoming or prom, but secretly promiscuous on the side. A smart person, but with lousy grades. A woman in possession of a jogging stride Allie had spent a lifetime trying to emulate, but without the least interest in joining the track team, in joining any team. In these ways Sonia had always been casual with herself, careless even, but never with others, and never so reckless with her own life as to engender real concern in family and friends.

Allie flipped through the book to a page where Andrew had left one of the twins' holographic bookmarks. *Chapter 7: It Wasn't Your Fault.*

The train lurched into a lower gear as a decaying campus of stone buildings drifted past the windows, an old but regal-looking penitentiary, like a forsaken college. She imagined him—the man who killed her sister—getting out of jail someday and living the rest of his life just fine, maybe even making his incarceration into a point of distinction on his résumé. *After my time at the University of Chicago but before my tenure at Grassland, I got into business junking cars.* That was about all she knew of him, that he'd gone to a nice college. An older couple on their block had a daughter who'd known him there. A years-ago economics class together, something. Others around Tower Hill knew him more directly. Friendly. Soft-spoken. Sober even.

She turned around to check on the Mennonites, who'd taken off their brimmed hats and fake sideburns and were looking out the window at a teenage boy standing on the train platform in dirt-smudged coveralls, holding a sign reading ALISON CRANE.

//

"I'm Allie."

The boy with the sign bowed slightly, then tossed the cardboard placard onto the train tracks. "Welcome to Wicklow." He appeared to be about sixteen, with messy hair and a copper bullet casing hanging from a leather necklace. "Victor couldn't make it," he explained. "So I'm supposed to take you to the grave."

Allie looked down at her shoes, lifting one to glance at the bottom.

"It's me you're smelling," the boy said. "We got a fertilizer delivery this morning. I didn't have time to change. Victor's been real distracted lately, so we're all pulling extra weight." He then led the way to a green pickup with a large plastic drum in the truck bed half full of an amber liquid.

Inside the truck, taped to the dashboard, was a page torn from a field guide with sketches of male and female oak slayer beetles. Allie recognized them from home, the shiny gray bugs whose boreholes bled a rusty brown discharge.

A month earlier, a trimming service had cut down the oak from the front yard of Allie's childhood home. In the wake of Sonia's death, her parents had sold the house and moved into a retirement community near the Wisconsin border. The new owners immediately painted the house yellow and removed the sickly tree. Allie had wanted to cry watching the oak being brought down, but the twins were in the car with her and the tears weren't coming anyway. "Girls," she'd simply said as the crane lowered a massive limb onto the driveway, "your aunt and I used to swing from that branch right there."

"Did you say something?" the boy asked.

Allie motioned to the beetle pictures on the dashboard. "They've already killed most of our oak trees. Are they here too?"

The boy nodded as he drove. "But Victor's fighting them."

The depressed little town, as it tumbled by the passenger window, reminded Allie not of Sonia at all but of a more generic sadness she imagined all people from nice suburbs must feel when passing through such small places on the brink. It was like looking into a cave and seeing one's ancient forebears, hairy and heavy of brow.

The boy paused at a traffic signal at the center of town. There was a motel on one side, a pharmacy on the other.

"Planned Parenthood," the boy said, jutting his chin at the building on the far side of the intersection. "My stepmom says all the pregnant college girls from Middle-Western go there."

"My sister went there," Allie said. "To Middle-Western, I mean." She looked at the clinic, which had a bright blue-tiled roof like a pancake house. "Is Victor going to meet me at the cemetery?"

"Don't know," said the boy. "Victor doesn't tell me much. I've only been working for him for a few months."

The light turned and the truck lurched forward, the amber liquid sloshing in the drum behind them.

"Can I ask," said Allie, "why you work at a cemetery?"

"There isn't much other work around here. In Triton there is, but you have to be twenty-one to work at the riverboat."

His face grew more solemn. "Plus, Victor pays me extra to stay late and keep people from jumping the fence."

"Does that happen a lot?"

"Uh-huh."

"What do they do when they get in?"

"You'll see in a minute." The boy pulled the truck through a wrought-iron gate bearing the sign OAK HILL CEMETERY, across a small parking lot and onto a narrow gravel lane heading up a wide slope full of large gravestones, statues, and mausoleums. Near a ten-foot obelisk, the boy jumped on the brake and hopped out to pick up a dead bird and toss it into the back of the truck. They continued down into a lower, shadier pasture with smaller markers, where he stopped again and led the way across the grass to a modest brown headstone supporting a can of Old Style. The boy scrambled ahead to snatch the beer can off the stone, and then to retrieve a smaller bit of trash from the grass at the base of the marker.

"What's this?" Allie asked.

"They *always* sneak in on Saturday nights," the boy complained. "This was actually kind of a light trashing." He motioned to a spot of charred turf. "Last weekend someone burned an effigy."

"This grave belongs to someone named Janice Page," said Allie.

"You'd think getting murdered would be insult enough," the boy said. "By a serial killer no less."

"This isn't the right grave."

The boy looked at the bit of garbage in his hand, at what appeared to be a condom wrapper. "Victor said to take you to *the* grave."

"With capital letters."

"What?"

"Sonia Lowery Senn," Allie said. "Can you please take me to *her* grave?"

"Senn? Like Victor Senn?"

"Yes. Can you take me to Victor's wife's grave?"

The boy looked at the condom wrapper again, then back up at Allie. "I didn't know Victor had a wife."

//

Near the administration building they got out to peruse a big directory of plots.

"I'm really sorry," the boy kept saying. "I just assumed that *the* grave meant *the grave*. But Jesus, I didn't know Victor's wife died. A year ago? Today?"

"She was my younger sister."

"No wonder he was acting so weird this morning."

"It's not listed here," said Allie. "How can that be?"

"I've never actually seen anyone update this thing," the boy admitted. "What about the burial? Weren't you here for that?"

Allie turned and looked up the long green slope dotted with headstones and hundred-year-old trees. "It was a bit of a blur."

The boy looked up the slope too. His eyes narrowed, and he stalked off to lift something—a dead robin—out of the grass beneath an angel statue.

"Why are there so many dead birds lying around?" Allie asked.

The boy tossed the robin into the truck bed. "Let me take you somewhere while I figure this out."

//

Motel Wicklow might've felt more homey and nostalgic—with its wood paneling and tube TV, as if drawn unchanged from Allie's childhood memories of family road trips—had it not apparently staged so many desperate lives. The smoked drapes, flecks of vomit on the underside of the toilet seat, a burned spoon in the waste bin. Residue of self-destructive crime.

Allie suddenly wanted to go jogging, but she hadn't brought any clothes for it, or any clothes at all that she wasn't already wearing. Lying on the moth-eaten bedcover listening to the distant commotion of Wicklow, she felt as if she were herself a criminal, or about to become one. Already on the run from her family, in a room rented by the hour, she would do something terrible soon, something wild and unforgivable. She closed her eyes, trying to imagine what it would be, but instead of the future, the tragic past approached—*We're entitled to a girls' night out, Sonia.* Outside, the myriad sounds of Wicklow converged into the singular redundant clanking of a tool striking iron, and she could hear again Mr. Bello fixing the playroom radiator. She could smell the pizza that Andrew and the kids were going to eat. She could hear her sister hedging on the other end of the line—*I'm waylaid, Al. I'm hurrying.* Allie had glanced at her watch. *Well, hurry faster,* she'd said. But Sonia never arrived. And then the night was over and the year had passed and there was only the clanking of a metal cup on jail bars, the killer hunched on a cot in his university sweatshirt with Allie in the top bunk, the two of them locked away together, rapping off the seconds of their tenured guilt, killers and victims both, until the clanking traded its metallic chime for the duller knock of knuckle on wood, and she was awake again in a motel room in Wicklow.

/,

"Victor?" she said, opening the door. "Victor, God, you look like shit."

He wore the same kind of coveralls as the boy with the bullet necklace, a bandolier of mud smeared across the torso, tobacco in his cheek, forehead jeweled with sweat. Not quite a full year since she'd seen him last, but he'd lost a decade to his grief. His thick hair had grown gray and frazzled, his eyes gaunt and staring, like some withering former alpha male excommunicated from the pack. He invited himself into one of the chairs by the window.

"Sorry about the mix-up," he said. "It's not Gunner's fault."

Allie took the chair opposite. "Gunner?"

He tongued his tobacco from one cheek to the other. "What are you doing here, Allie?"

"Not sure," she said, looking around the room. "I think I may be leaving my husband or something."

Victor rolled his eyes. "Does Andrew know that?"

"I just thought of it this minute," she said. "It's this anniversary. My mind isn't right. But he drinks these kale shakes and—"

"Kale?"

"It's a vegetable."

"This is Andrew we're talking about."

"And he reads these stupid self-help books."

Victor smirked. "You're not leaving Andrew. You're just pitying yourself."

"You don't know what I'm going through."

"Sure I do," he said. "Same as me. You're completely fucked in the head."

Allie looked out across the street at the pharmacy. "I told her to hurry up."

"Told who?"

"On the night," she said. "We were supposed to go to that concert, remember, and I told Sonia to hurry up. She was driving fast because of me."

"She got killed by a drunk driver, Allie."

"How are *you* so cool about all this?"

"Because I already talked myself off the ledge this morning," he said. "This is the good part of my day. This is the part *after* I've decided not to drive off a cliff."

"Don't joke about that, Victor."

"I'm not joking, Allie. On the way to work every morning, I pass an old quarry with cliffs all around it. The guardrail isn't much to speak of. It would be a quick way to go." He looked away, his eyes softening as he watched the traffic go past. "But then I make it past the one really sharp curve, and I'm still on the road, so I end up going to work. Dig a few graves, bury a few bodies, then off to happy hour with June."

"June?"

"Don't say it like that," he said.

"Like what?"

"Like you think I'm screwing her."

"*Are* you screwing her?"

"No, I was just saying . . ." He sleeved off his forehead. "It was a figure of speech."

Allie straightened her posture. "So who *is* June then?"

He eyed her, apparently trying to discern whether to validate her new tone with a response. "June runs the cemetery office in my continuing psychological absence."

"And is that June's phrase for your being"—she touched her chin—"'fucked in the head'?"

"It's actually my therapist's."

"Oh, good for you," she said, slipping back into the tone he didn't like.

"It's not really therapy. It's just a neighbor of mine who happens to *be* a therapist."

"Well, either way, Andrew would approve. He's been after me to see someone too. But he's been after me to do a million things." She reached into her purse and took out *So You're Grieving, Now What?*, used it to fan her face, then threw it onto the table. "But I don't do anything these days. I don't even run anymore. I mean I *want* to take a run, and sometimes I even get my shoes on, but then, I don't know, I just don't do it."

"Psychological absence," said Victor.

Allie nodded. "I'm calling it a life of refusal. I'm thinking of joining up with the Mennonites." She looked out the window at the pharmacy across the street. "I think it would make a nice distraction."

Victor pulled the self-help book off the table and thumbed through the pages, stopping at the bookmark. "Would you like to see something?" he asked.

"What?"

"My number one distraction," he said.

"Screwing June?"

"Better than that."

"What is it?"

"It's the war I'm waging," he said. "Come on."

11

As darkness began to descend on Oak Hill Cemetery, Victor keyed in through the big iron gate. They wound their way up a wide slope of gravestones, the drum of amber liquid in the truck bed sloshing behind them. The male and female beetle pictures fluttered beneath the air vents as if whispering to one another.

Victor tapped the brake, dodging a mound of feathers in the middle of the drive.

"What's with all the dead animals?" Allie asked.

Victor drew a small metal box from beneath his seat. It had a single red button on top with two wires trailing into the crevice between his seat and the console. "The birds," he said. "Yeah. Sometimes they get themselves caught in the chemistry."

They crested the hill and he pulled over. She followed him out of the truck to the base of a massive tree. "Northern red oak," he announced. "This right here is the biggest oak tree in the entire county." Victor opened the blade of a pocketknife, stripped off a chunk of bark, sniffed it, and handed it to Allie. "Smell that?"

It smelled like bark.

"Oak slayers," he hissed. "Those little fuckers can smell an old tree like this from a hundred miles away." He was staring intensely at the trunk now, his shoulders lifting and falling. The darkness was gathering fast. "They mate for life, you know. They fall in love and then they pick a tree and chew their way into the heartwood. And then they just shack up and eat, and their larvae eat. For years this goes on, multiplying and eating. They never even leave the tree, some of them.

They're so safe in there, deep inside the bigger trees especially, that the woodpeckers can't even get to them. Until it's completely empty inside." Victor looked up into the darkening sky. He appeared to Allie, standing there in his dirty coveralls with the darkness folding around him, like a convict on the run, desperate and dangerous.

Back in the truck, they sat in silence. Victor put the keys in the ignition, but didn't turn the engine on. He put his hands in his lap.

"I noticed you're not wearing your wedding ring anymore," she said quietly.

He set his chin on the steering wheel, scanning the sky.

"What are we doing now?" she asked.

"We're waiting," he said.

"For what?"

"For total darkness."

Allie cupped her hands against the window. The silhouette of a bat swung across the slightly less dark sky. "Total darkness," she agreed. "It does feel that way sometimes, like we're just waiting for the end."

"No," he said, thumbing back toward the drum in the truck's bed. "The pesticide. It's sort of a gray-market kind of thing. Developed the recipe myself. I only distribute it under cover of darkness." He turned the key. The beetle pictures began whispering beneath the vents again. "While I drive," he said, setting the wired box on her thigh, "you count to tens. At every ten, push that button." He reached across and dropped his fist on the button and Allie could hear a hissing sound. Beyond the rear window, a plume of yellow mist drifted off the back end of the drum, turning red in the brake lights.

"What is that?" she asked.

He threw the truck into gear and guided it out from under the great oak.

Allie turned to watch the yellow cloud swirl and eddy in their wake. "Seriously, what is that stuff?"

"Go on, try it," he said, reaching across to nudge the metal box on her thigh. "Conventional grief management it ain't, but it just feels good to waste those little fuckers."

Allie put the metal box into the cup holder.

"Suit yourself." Victor pulled up along the crest of the hill and down a wide grassy lane between rows of headstones, a grim poise ossifying his face. He punched the button again. Behind them another plume burst from the drum in a powered stream, then churned downward, settling in a low stationary cloud. Back and forth across the slope, every ten seconds he reached down to press the button himself, until finally they were out on the street again, zipping down the dark roads of Wicklow, the metal box back up under the seat.

//

"I don't understand," said Andrew, his voice meek with concern as it came through the old phone in her motel room. "Then when *are* you coming home?" Perhaps he sensed it too, the precriminal vibe his wife was giving off. He'd been to Wicklow before, after all. A place with some country charm in daylight, but with a despondent kind of nightlife that Andrew once described as a "hobo jubilee." Years ago, they'd eaten dinner at Sonia and Victor's house to celebrate the acquisition of the cemetery, before going out to a bar near Oak Hill. A dark, wet-smelling dive like a basement exhumed to ground level.

"I'll come home tomorrow," Allie said, turning the rings on her finger. "I haven't seen it yet. Seen her. There was this kid named Gunner, with a bullet around his neck, and he took me to the wrong grave, and after that I fell asleep, and then the day was over."

"Allie," Andrew asked, "are you drunk?"

"Not yet," she said. "I'm thinking of going to the bar across the street, or the pharmacy, for some wine maybe. But everything in the window is in jugs. You know, with the round handles? It's worse than before, this place. Like they only have stuff to outfit the goners. Nothing but jug wine and condoms and charred spoons."

"Spoons?" he said.

Allie stood up off the bed and glanced into the waste bin to see the blackened piece of metal. In her life she'd never seen a thing like that and here she was so casually remarking on it. When she eventually returned home to the big house her husband had bought for her she would snap out of this dream and say—her own voice meek with concern—"Oh my God, Andrew, there was a heroin spoon in my room!" And then Andrew would mention a news item he'd seen about the growing epidemic, and they'd be together again, sharing similar thoughts, in their Tower Hill home where the wine bottles lived in cellars and the spoons were all silver.

"Is Victor doing all right?" he asked.

"Oh, he's doing fine," she said. "He's keeping himself distracted with a spraying campaign. You remember how much he worried over his trees."

"What do you mean by 'spraying campaign'?"

She thought of the poisonous yellow fog they'd draped over the cemetery, of the vacant expression Victor had worn as the songbirds dropped from the trees in their wake. And as she reconsidered her husband's question—*Is Victor doing all right?*— she understood that she would never see her brother-in-law again.

"Anyway," she continued, "it's admirable the way Victor's trying to save his trees from the beetles. It's constructive, I mean. Maybe *I* should be saving something. The whales, maybe. Is there a five-K for that? I really felt like running today, for the whales. Or maybe for the men who keep jumping off that one Metra platform . . ." She could hear herself rambling, her voice tightening inside her throat, the words coming out in a tense key. "Anyway, I'll visit the grave in the morning, and if Victor's up for it maybe he'll come too."

"Up for it?" Andrew asked. "I thought he was doing 'fine.'" His voice seemed to have swallowed itself too, as if it came now from a great distance. Or, it was right there in her ear, but muted, as if he were speaking behind one of those thick glass panels at a prison. And then it struck her—the seedy motel room, the long-distance call—she was ending her marriage. She wasn't ever going home. Tomorrow she would say goodbye to her sister and then she'd buy up all the jerky at the pharmacy and head west to the mountains. Or south, maybe, to Mexico. Or Canada. Where were the beetles coming from? She would run away from the beetles, to someplace that still had its oak trees. They'd come from the east, she decided, from Amish country. A big red arrow across the continent on a news report, stabbing into the Midwest, like a map of the rust belt or the spread of heroin.

"What?" Andrew asked.

"Did I say something?"

"You said 'jerky.'"

"Did I?" she asked. "Maybe. Yeah. It's this motel room, it reminds me of the road trips we used to take as kids. My dad always bought us beef jerky at the gas stations."

Andrew began talking again, about the things he'd learned from the book he'd planted in her purse, which Allie had already ditched in the bedside drawer where the Bible should've been. He was talking but she wasn't hearing it. And as he droned on about the power of self-forgiveness, she reached into the waste bin and lifted the spoon to her face, staring at her dark and distorted reflection in the charred metal oval.

//

In the morning, the bedside phone rang. It was Gunner. He was coming over to pick up Allie for another try at the grave.

"You spoke with Victor?" Allie asked. "This morning?"

"He didn't come into work," Gunner said. "But I spoke with June. And June knows where the bodies are buried. So get ready, I'm coming over."

The boy was there in minutes. His hair had been combed backward and he'd buttoned himself into a white shirt and slacks.

"He's not poisoning the town or anything," Gunner explained as he drove. "June says Victor used to be a chemist before he bought the cemetery. It's true that the birds are taking it hard, but if Oak Hill loses its oak trees, then what will it have?"

The sun was shining in through Allie's side of the car, stoking something mean inside her head, like a hangover except she hadn't drunk anything. "The grave you took me to yesterday, was that woman really murdered by a serial killer?"

"The Soyfield Strangler," Gunner said. "It was never proved that it was actually his handiwork, but it wasn't *dis*proved either."

The downtown strip fell away and they passed through blocks of tired housing. The bright morning light was trying to make the place charming again, but it wasn't working.

"What about you?" Gunner asked. "Does anything exciting ever happen where you're from?"

Allie thought of the intersection where Sonia had been killed, the piles of flowers that accumulated afterward. She thought of the Metra station where the depressed commuters were stepping in front of trains, the haunted reputation it was gaining. She said, "Can I tell you something? About Victor?"

The boy pulled through Oak Hill's parking lot. "Okay."

"He's sleeping with this June person. Did you know that?"

Gunner glanced at her. The car drifted, then abruptly found the lane again. "I don't know," he said. "I guess, maybe I knew. I mean, I suppose I thought it was *possible*."

"I figured you did. You're a sharp kid. I can tell. Okay, well, you should let this slide. For Victor's sake. It's an awkward thing to have the boss being intimate with one employee, especially if there are promotions and bonuses and stuff available. There's a fear of favoritism. But Victor's in a bad place right now. He's all messed up in the head, so you can't call him out on something like that, or else—" A large black bat lay on the stoop of a mausoleum, wings spread wide as if it had perished midflight.

The boy shook his head, mouthing words to himself.

"This June person," Allie continued. "It's Victor just blowing off some steam. He needs this right now, or else—"

Gunner swerved around a pair of doves on the pavement.

"He just needs this one distraction, is all. It's important. Or else—"

"You keep saying 'or else,'" the boy said. "Or else *what*?"

"I don't know," said Allie. "It's possible he poses some kind of danger to himself, I guess. It's a traumatic thing to lose someone you love. He needs people around him who are going to be understanding for a while. Do you think you can do that?"

The boy angled the truck down into a shaded meadow surrounded by oak trees. He stopped the truck, glaring into the center of the steering wheel. Finally, he cleared his throat and said in a quiet voice, "June is my stepmother."

"Oh," said Allie. "Like she's your . . ."

"My dad's wife."

"Oh," she said again. "I see. Okay, well, maybe you're not the person I'm supposed to be talking to about this."

"Maybe not," the boy agreed, his eyes still boring into the steering wheel.

"It's possible, too, that I'm wrong."

Gunner pointed straight ahead. "The grave's over there."

Allie watched the boy a moment longer, then got out. As she walked, she expected to hear Gunner take off in the truck, but there were only the sounds of the wind and crickets and a highway shushing in the distance beyond a row of willow trees. And then there it was in front of her, the stone she hadn't been able to conjure in her memory. SONIA LOWERY SENN. A simple stone after all. Gray, not big, not small. A reasonable, self-assured monument. Self-possessed. What had she been expecting? To hate the stone and have Victor to blame? To love it and feel joy at its rightness? But it was only a stone, similar to some others around. She stood and stared, trying to have a certain feeling about it, about her sister being beneath it, about anything. A feeling to indulge or refuse. A distraction, a catharsis, anything. And then, as she waited for something to occur to her, as she ran up and down the aisles of her memory, she found herself coming suddenly back into the present, her mind emptying out and her eyes tracking something real instead, *on* the stone, a shiny little coin tramping across Sonia's name.

//

Inside the administration building, a short woman in a skirt suit came rushing out of an office to meet them. She had blond bangs and a sharply upturned nose, a dappling of crumbs on her navy-blue blouse. One look at the beetle in Gunner's hands and the blood left her face. She dumped her uneaten sandwich into the waste bin and teased the creature into the empty ziplock.

"Where the hell is Victor?" Gunner asked her.

The woman ran to her desk phone and frantically dialed a number. "Victor," she shouted. "Jesus Christ, Vic, it's June. We've got an oak slayer on the property. Call me back right now."

"'Vic'?" the boy asked, his eyes darting around his step-mother's office. "Since when do you call him *Vic*?"

June stared back at him, her eyes ballooning in the sockets. "He became Vic when I realized we don't have any time to waste here. Now call your father and tell him you're gonna be late tonight."

Gunner reached for the phone on her desk, but she snatched it away and dialed another number, listened, shook her head.

Then she hung up and turned, finally, to Allie. "Who the hell are you?"

"I'm Victor's sister-in-law."

This information seemed to neither surprise nor impress June, who swiped the crumbs off her blouse and said, "Cemetery's closed. I'm taking you to the train station. Gunner, lock the gate behind us. Victor's gonna want to spray."

"He already sprayed last night," said Allie.

June, who'd started toward the door, turned abruptly, putting her huge eyes on Allie now. "Well, dear, he's gonna want to spray again."

"In the middle of the day?" Gunner asked. He looked at the phone again. Everyone did. It didn't ring.

⁄⁄

June's Cherokee was a mess of fast-food wrappers and parking tickets. A sun-damaged photo of a red-bearded man who must've been Gunner's cuckolded father peered up from the cup holder. June drove leaning forward, hanging on to the wheel. She might've been prettier, Allie thought, if not so angry looking. Allie imagined there was a large handgun in this woman's purse, in her glove compartment, under the driver's seat maybe. It was possible Victor had been kidding about sleeping with this woman. Allie hoped, now, that it wasn't true, though she couldn't decide what stakes her mind had been attaching to the possibility. She tried to imagine Victor in this woman's hard embrace. Then she thought of him folded up inside the gnarled burning wreck of his truck.

"Don't start worrying about him now," June said as she

pulled into the train station parking lot. "Victor will figure this out. He'll be fine."

Allie checked her phone. She'd dialed Victor three times on the way to the station. No answer. No calls back.

June stopped the truck in front of the stairway heading up to the platform. The train rumbled closer from an unseen distance.

"Do *you* think he's okay?" Allie knew it now, as the words left her mouth, that he was already dead somewhere. Hanging from a well-loved oak maybe, or bleeding out inside the crushed cab of his spray truck at the bottom of the quarry. Or, if he wasn't dead yet, he would be soon, one way or another. A man waiting for total darkness. "I could stay if you guys need me to help with something."

June shook her head. "I don't want this to sound mean," she said, "but having you here is making Victor completely fucking insane." She paused to consider these words, or perhaps it was the train's distance she was trying to gauge, wondering how much longer she'd have to endure the presence of this wealthy grief-wounded woman in her car, in her town. "That did sound mean, didn't it? I'm sorry, dear. None of this is your fault."

//

As the Prairie Stater carried her away, Allie decided it felt good to be leaving Wicklow even if the idea of returning home didn't. There were Amish on board again, or Mennonites. Something. But they were real this time. Their faith in refusal was authentic, Allie could tell.

She glanced at her phone again. How many times per minute must she send her mind flying off the edge of that quarry with poor Victor? His grief was greater than hers, she realized, more damaging, more isolating. She checked her phone one last time, then turned it off. A minor relief pulsed through her as the screen went black. Why is it, she wondered, that the pain of others makes us feel less stricken?

//

In the city, she changed trains, back in Tower Hill by mid-afternoon, getting off one station early at the platform where the depressed commuters were throwing themselves away. She stood there for a time staring at the tracks, indulging the ghosts of their greater pain.

Then the long walk home, past the houses of friends, past the downtown full of boutiques and salons, past the Spot where Sonia had died.

"Allie," Andrew said, gasping her name. The children, oblivious until that moment, appeared to fill suddenly with the anxiety their father was exhaling. "I've been calling and calling," he said. "I thought you'd have been home hours ago."

"I got off at the wrong station," she said. "My phone was off. I needed to take a walk."

"A walk?" he said, his voice bending with curiosity.

"What are you guys doing?" Allie shed her purse, her shoes. Her family was at the dining room table huddled around a big plastic cylinder. "Is that . . . Is that your old food dehydrator?"

Andrew smiled sheepishly. "You said 'jerky' last night on the phone and it got me thinking we should make some." He looked down at the mess they'd made—strips of raw meat lined up on a serving platter, the girls' initials drawn in drifts of spilled salt. "I kinda *miss* jerky," he said.

Allie came around the table to hug the twins, still in their pajamas. They'd all stayed home, they reported gleefully, on a Monday, just because. Andrew was wearing the sweatpants Allie had bought him years ago so they could run together. So she could have someone to run with when they still lived in the city in the crappy neighborhood. So she could have someone there beside her to talk to and to listen to also—his stomach cramp complaints, his shin splints, his possibly collapsing arches—someone there who was suffering just a little bit worse than you.

BEFORE THE RUST

As Rick LaForge pulled up in front of his best friend's house, the curtains split open and Janice Page's face appeared. A miracle, he thought. Time and tragedy undone. But then the fantasy broke apart and Rick understood what he was really seeing.

Glennis in her thirties had become an identical twin to her mother's final self. The same darkened eyes, the same long hair framing that blameless pout. Rick hadn't seen much of her in adulthood. Distance was best, he'd decided long ago, as nothing good had ever come of his attempts to help her out in the past. With her husband in Grassland up the road, she'd come back to Wicklow to live with her father, and this had led Rick to avoid Emmit too, in what turned out to be the man's final years.

He stepped out of his car and waved.

Glennis pressed her middle finger against the glass.

By the time he'd let himself in with the key beneath the mat, she'd vacated the front room, leaving a long crooked dent in the couch cushions. The coffee table was littered with empty bottles of tonic water.

"Glennis," he called out, "I'm only here to check on you."
A toilet flushed.

"I know you're sad right now," he continued loudly, "and
I'm not gonna hang around and try to make you feel better if
it's alone time you're looking for . . ."

A door squeaked, footsteps padded closer. She appeared in
the kitchen doorway, blinking through her hangover. "So,"
she said, "what are they saying?"

"Saying?" he asked. "Who?"

"People."

"What people?"

"The townspeople, Rick. The people of Wicklow. What
are they saying about my dad?"

"It's only been a day," he said. "And besides, there's nothing
to say. Nothing bad, I mean. What's to say? He lived a decent
life, it should've been better."

"That's quite a eulogy." She turned back into the kitchen.

"Wait," he said. "I came here to help."

Glennis pulled several juice containers out of the refriger-
ator and set them onto the counter. "I don't need *help,* Rick."

"I'm talking about with the funeral arrangements."

"Oh." She closed the fridge and leaned against it. "Yeah,
okay."

"Do you think your dad wanted one?"

"One what?"

"A funeral, Glen. Christ, go back to sleep if you're still
drunk."

Glennis winced. "Okay, let me think. A funeral. I don't
know. What if we just did something small, here at the house?"

"Then a burial?" he asked.

She sighed, looked at the ceiling.

"What is it?" he asked.

"Umm, nothing. Never mind. A burial, yeah. He should be next to my mother."

"I'll take care of it," Rick said. "But you've got to pull yourself together."

She gathered up her juice cartons and carried them into the front room, where she lay back down on the couch and turned on the TV.

"You're gonna need to clean yourself up *a little* for this." He stood staring at her, listening to the TV stutter through channels. "Are you listening to me, Glennis? Are you hearing this?"

//

As he pulled into the cemetery, Rick couldn't help but recall the speculation that had seized Wicklow in the wake of Janice's death three decades earlier. He'd felt their stares during her funeral, those supposed friends and neighbors, heard them whispering during the burial service. For months the rumors persisted, for years. It was possible that some still wondered about him. People believed what they wanted to believe. If they'd witnessed your last-second touchdown pass in the state quarterfinals, then you received the benefit of doubts. If they could imagine you'd one day return to Wicklow to help stave off economic annihilation, then they thought twice about joining the chorus of rumors. But if all they remembered was that you'd dated Janice Page in high school and that after she dumped you for your best friend you carved her initials deep into both your biceps, then you were a pathetic lovelorn murderer.

"Can I help you?" an unseen voice barked.

Rick shuffled across the marble floor of the cemetery's administration building and peered into an office.

A small, fierce-looking woman in a skirt suit looked up from her desk. She pointed at Rick and said, "I've been expecting you."

"You have?"

"Sure. You're here to bury your pal."

"Emmit Page," he said. "His wife's already here. Buried, I mean."

"Oh, I'm aware."

Rick swallowed. "Do teenagers still leave graffiti on the headstone?"

"And beer bottles and condoms and Ouija boards and—"

"It's a shame," said Rick.

A hollow smile creased the woman's face. "You have no idea where the shame ends."

"Pardon?"

"I can't let your friend in here," she said. "Not even for the great quarterback."

"Look . . ." He located a nameplate amid the clutter of her desk. "Look, June, it's not Emmit's fault that a bunch of teenagers—"

"It's not that," she said. "I just can't allow it. Not in a million years. Emmit Page's son-in-law killed Victor's wife."

"Who's Victor?"

"Victor's the boss," she said. "He owns the cemetery. I heard the news about your pal this morning and I've been waiting all day long for you to roll in here to ask me the stupidest question ever."

Rick scratched his head. "I didn't know any of this."

"I suppose I believe you," she said.

"But it's just that his wife's already buried here, and—"

"You're really still asking me this?" She spoke loudly as if there were others in the room to hear it. "After what I just told you?"

"I knew Glennis's husband was in jail for *something*."

"Ve*hic*ular *man*slaughter."

"Yes but—"

"But you understand now," she said, her voice turning almost peppy, "that we're done discussing this matter?"

"I'm just trying to put the guy in the ground."

"Ricky?" she asked. "Is it still Ricky?"

"It's Rick now."

"Ricky," she said, "honestly, it's your truly terrific luck that my boss isn't here right now to hear you prattle on about how we should help out your pal whose lush of a daughter is married to the piece of shit who killed Sonia."

Rick heard footsteps. He turned to see a young man in a Middle-Western shirt coming down the hall.

"I know it's not your fault, sweetie," June continued. "But that's probably why the good Lord timed it this way, so that I don't have to watch you send Victor into yet another grief spiral. It's miraculous timing, almost like that famous throw you made to your pal."

The college boy appeared at Rick's side. This was a kid with some muscles hidden underneath the beer meat. He put his hand around Rick's upper arm, his fingers pressing into the old self-inflicted scars. "Time's up, dude." And then they scuffled their way across the lobby, before Rick straightened his jacket and walked out on his own. He was still coming out of this daze the whole walk back to the car, sucking oxygen, cursing the woman and the college boy and the whole shitty way his best friend's life was turning out even after it was over.

"This goddamn town," he said to the bartender. "I've been trying so hard to make it a bigger place, but it's still such a podunk shithole." He went on about his attempts to improve Wicklow, about his now-scuttled venture into affordable housing, about his subsequent conversion of the burned-down trailer park into a postapocalyptic paintball arena, and about his newest effort to repurpose the mill into an even bigger paintball venue.

"I can't imagine," the bartender said, "why people don't appreciate you turning our disasters into playgrounds." Rick hated this man, the way he'd wincingly smile each time he refilled a glass. But then, seven drinks later, Rick didn't hate anyone anymore, not even the awful bitch at the cemetery. What he did hate was how rapidly his drunkenness had come on, as if the dizzying rage he'd felt when the college boy grabbed his arm had made him weak to the booze, and now he was stuck here, miles from his house, too drunk to drive home, and drinking more still, trapped and joyless.

"Is that what this is?" he moaned. He was in the bathroom now, retching into the urinal. The bartender had a portable phone to his ear, saying, "Yes, as soon as possible, yes, the quarterback, uh-huh, going to the mansion on Hill Road."

"How the hell do you know where I live?" Rick shouted. But there was no real surprise in it, nor any alarm when a team of strangers helped him so gently off the floor and out to the waiting cab.

//

"My name is Rick . . ." he said in the morning, wearing his hangover like a pale stinking mask, "and I'm an alcoholic."

"Hello Rick."

"It's been eleven hours since my last drink . . ."

Someone in the back groaned, a female voice he couldn't place in the blurry crowd. "I didn't mean for it to happen," he went on, "but I lost my best friend yesterday, and the cemetery won't bury him, and it's harder than you'd think to get investors on board with an apocalyptic motif . . ."

Afterward, Angela the mother of two with the jean jacket approached with a plate of Oreos. Every week after the formal session they stood together and kept a quiet, unpausing conversation. Anything not to be alone in that underground room in the community center.

"Were you the one groaning?" he asked her.

Angela waved her hand dismissively at the rest of the room. "Eleven hours of sobriety isn't so bad," she said. "It's much worse if you can't come in and admit to only eleven hours. You're already back on the wagon, Rick. You're fine." She nodded sternly. "But what's this about your friend?"

"Long story."

"He died?"

"Maybe it's shorter than I thought."

"This was the guy with throat cancer?"

He took a cookie off her plate and tried to explain. Angela came from someplace else—Indiana or Iowa—so it was all new to her, the story of Janice's murder, the years of Emmit living in infamy, the troubles Glennis had found in her own life.

"Oh sure, I've seen the wife's grave," Angela said. "I take walks through Oak Hill sometimes. The teenagers. Jesus. What the hell is wrong with people?" She downed her coffee then glared hatefully into the empty paper cup. "I don't know, maybe the rust is to blame."

"The rust?" Rick asked.

"All these cancers going around. I feel like it must be all the rust, and the runoff. Like it's gotten into the groundwater. Nothing but oxidation and decay. There's your apocalyptic motif." Angela shook her head, then looked at him more forcefully. "Cremation," she said. "Trust me."

"I don't know."

"Your friend, he wanted depraved teenagers humping all over his final resting place too?"

Over Angela's shoulder, Rick watched a pair of men chatting with a younger woman. Her back was to him, but her body made a nice shape under the sweatshirt.

Angela shuffled into his line of sight. "You need to get past this, Rick, and quick. Or else you're gonna be in here eleven hours later every day this week. Burn him, scatter him, move on."

The young woman in the sweatshirt excused herself from her conversation and drifted toward the table of refreshments. She moved her hand over the plates, touching cookies and pretzels, then deciding against them. Finally, she put her hand into a bowl of crackers, lifting one to her face.

Janice.

//

"You could've warned me about the cemetery," Rick said as he put his car in gear.

Glennis drew her seat belt across her torso, then decided against it. "I was pretty out of it yesterday."

"And today—what? You're sober?"

"I do appreciate you *trying* to arrange it." Her voice sounded washed out, almost kindly in its exhaustion. "I do wish we could bury him with my mom."

"Well, trust me," he said, "it's not gonna happen."

Glennis held the last nub of a cracker in her fingers. As the car picked up speed, she rolled down the window and set it free.

"Isn't there a Bohemian cemetery out on the state highway?" he asked.

Glennis shrugged.

"What about cremation?" he asked.

She rolled the window back up.

"No?"

"I'm thinking," she said.

"We could scatter the ashes, at the quarry maybe. Just you and me."

"The quarry?"

"Your dad and I used to hang out there as kids. Everyone did. We threw parties there, after big games. It was a special place. It was where cheerleaders lost their virginity to football players."

Glennis unzipped her purse. "I lost my virginity to an apocalyptic paintball entrepreneur."

"Jesus, Glen—" He took his foot off the pedal as they approached the intersection at the center of town, Motel Wicklow slowing down on their left. "I don't know. We'll scatter him *somewhere*. The point is I don't think your dad would be served by a bunch of people standing around talking about him while, you know, trying *not* to talk about him."

Glennis looked at the motel. "I have such a headache."

"It goes away eventually," Rick explained. "I can coach you through the first few days of being clean, but what you really need is a sponsor."

"I'm not so sure about this."

He glanced sideways. "You're not sure about cremation or sobriety?"

The red light held them between the motel and the bar, with
no cars passing in the other direction. Glennis pulled a beer can
from her purse, snapped back the ring, and took a drink.

"Great, Glennis. I can tell you're really serious about your
sobriety."

"The light's green, Rick." As he accelerated down the road
she took a long drink and then another, tipping the can back
a half dozen times in a row and then dropping the empty into
the cup holder.

"Okay," she said, as they pulled up to her father's house. "I
think I can do it."

"Do what?"

"Yeah," she said. "I'll go along with it, but there's somewhere you've got to take me first. Tomorrow."

"What are you talking about, Glennis?"

"Cremation," she said. "You're right. It's the right thing
to do. Let's do it. Okay then. But first I need this one favor
from you."

//

Rick drove home and sat in the car in the garage with the engine off, smelling her boozy breath still inside the cabin, staring
at the gleaming dots of beer on the rim of the can, the prints
where her lips had touched the aluminum. He leaned over and
smelled the beer inside the can, the pooled glint of one last sip
lying at the bottom. He tried to shake off the urge. He was
being set up, he told himself. She was undermining him. She
was getting back at him. He pulled his hand away from the aluminum, crossed his arms. But then he felt again the raised scar
tissue on his biceps, the initials of his best friend's wife.

"But I didn't do it," he said to no one.

And no one listened.

He looked at the beer in the cup holder.

"Don't do it," he said.

He lifted the can.

He felt the tiny liquid weight inside.

//

On the way to his meeting the next morning Rick added up the hours since that sip. And then the smaller number of hours since he'd gone back into the car in the middle of the night to shake the last *last* drops of beer onto his tongue.

"Shit," he said, staying in the car, staring at the community center door. "Shit . . . Shit . . . Shit . . ." The whole hour slid by this way—cursing, radio on, radio off, his hand occasionally finding the door lever before pulling away again. It was Angela he couldn't face. Or perhaps she was the only one, and it was the rest of the room he feared. The door to the community center opened and the familiar faces made their way out into the parking lot. Then Glennis emerged.

"This isn't your meeting!" he shouted out the window as he swung his car up to the curb. "This is a meeting for people who actually want to get clean."

Glennis squinted into his car. "Rick?"

"This is *my* group, Glennis. And you're not even trying to be sober."

"I'm trying," she said in an unbothered voice. She was dressed up in a skirt and blouse, her hair down, makeup putting some color back into her face. "Anyway, where've *you* been?"

"I've been trying like hell not to drink."

"Yeah, I hear that." She tugged the door open and slid onto the passenger seat. "We can pick up the ashes this afternoon, but I need that favor first."

As they drove down the state route, Rick could feel his rage giving up on him. Glennis's touch with the radio felt oddly magical, transitioning from rock to bluegrass to a sensual electronica that ran a warm thumping knife under his ribs. He just drove and listened and let his mind go empty while she fidgeted with her bracelets, occasionally dipping her hand into her purse for a flask.

The prison appeared in the distance, the watchtowers first, then the concentric brambles of razor-wire fencing, the stretches of matted grasses in between, not yet recovered from the long winter.

"How long does this usually take?" he asked.

"There's a lot of waiting for doors to buzz open." She stiffened as the car nosed into the checkpoint. Rick expected her to do the talking, but she only grinned anxiously at the guard.

"Here to visit Hartley Nolan," Rick declared.

The guard said, "Didn't expect two of you."

"He's staying in the car," Glennis finally managed.

Rick parked at the edge of the lot where some hollowed tree segments had been piled beside a dwindling mound of gray snow. Glennis disappeared into the building. The radio turned stale. Commercials across the dial. The guard in the checkpoint hut came out onto the blacktop to look at a prop plane buzzing in the southern sky.

"Don't worry," the guard said, ranging closer. "They don't let 'em laze around afterward."

"Pardon?"

"The conjugal," the guard said. "They only get about forty-five minutes."

Eventually Glennis reappeared, the collar of her sweater turned under, her hair tied back in a ponytail. She got into the car without a word and they rode in silence back through downtown Triton, until he asked if she wanted to get lunch.

"I'm not hungry," she said. "But okay."

At a riverfront café near the casino, she ordered a gin and tonic as the maître d' handed out menus. When the waitress arrived, Glennis reordered the drink. Rick asked for a burger and an iced tea.

"Honestly, Glennis," he said as the waitress walked away, "it doesn't look like you're even trying."

"Can we fix me next week?"

"It doesn't work that way."

"It needs to," she said. "Right now it does. My husband's in a cage and my father's in an oven, so I could actually *use* this cocktail."

The waitress set the drinks in front of them, then scurried away.

Rick leaned forward. "Is this my fault, Glennis?"

"Is what your fault?"

"You," he said. "The state you're in. Am I the one who fucked you up?"

"That's an interesting choice of words."

"I'm not asking for forgiveness, Glen. I was a piece of shit back then. I was a drunk. But I do need to know how bad I'm supposed to feel. I need to know the toll I've taken."

Glennis took a long drink. "Did you know," she finally said, "that there are people in town who still think you killed my mother?"

"Rumors never die," he said, looking across the gray river at the big pink hotel. "I was on a submarine when it happened. It took a while for the police to figure that out, but *you* know that, right? That I was in the middle of the Atlantic Ocean? That I was *under* the Atlantic Ocean when it happened?"

"I know." Glennis reached for her drink again, but behind the glass he could see a reddening around her eyes. "And my dad was in Taiwan on business . . ." she added in a wearied voice, as if it were a school fact she'd been made to memorize.

"That's right," he said.

Tears squeezed from the corners of her eyes. "I know this is weird," she said, "but I sometimes wish someone who'd loved her *had* been the one to do it. For her sake, you know, not to have been so alone at the end." She tipped the glass back and back until the ice collapsed onto her face. Then she busied herself wiping her mouth and cheeks, her eyes. The food arrived and Glennis looked suddenly hungry, so he cut his burger in half and ordered her another cocktail, and then he drove her back to her father's house and he left her on the couch and went out and sat in his car in the driveway trying to conjure again the sight of Janice's face in that window.

//

The next day, he drove over to Emmit's house, where dozens of people had gathered. Some of Rick's old high school buddies were there, men he'd have nothing to say to that didn't revolve around two-a-days in August or last-second Hail Marys. A throng of Emmit's former co-workers mingled in the kitchen, and the dining room was full of women who'd worshipped Janice in high school, or hated her. Either way they'd have taken some satisfaction in her fall from grace, though he imagined the years since her murder would have dulled that cynicism into a cautionary tale they'd probably told their teenage daughters.

Glennis made her way over to Rick, towing a prim stylish couple she introduced as Hartley's parents. The mother wore black pearls. The stepfather was a man in pleated pants with a dapper Indian accent. They spoke kindly of Emmit, murmuring their sorrow upon hearing the news, remarking resignedly at how insufficiently they'd known him. Rick nodded and nodded. Glennis drifted off into the crowd.

"Tell us," Hartley's mother hissed as soon as her daughter-in-law was out of earshot, "is Glennis still drinking?"

Rick looked around the room. "She's certainly grieving, ma'am."

"Yes, but—"

There was a commotion in the living room, and the crowd hushed as Glennis climbed on top of a chair. "Thank you, everyone, for coming . . ." she said. Rick could feel the mother-in-law's attention still hanging on him, but he kept his eyes trained on Glennis. "My father was born here and he died here," she began. "But in between, he mostly stayed away. Early on, travel was just something a young salesman had to do. But later, when he could've taken up with the home office full-time, he stayed on the road for reasons I know you all can imagine. And later, when I began to grow up, he moved us away from Wicklow entirely." She crouched, then stood up again with a dark ceramic urn now in the crook of her arm. Seeing the urn himself—his best friend reduced to a pint of dust on the arm of a grieving drunk waif—Rick felt unsteady too.

". . . Why my father then chose to come *back* to Wicklow," Glennis continued, "I'll never know, except that he loved this

town, and I think he wanted to outlive the notoriety. I wish
he had." She turned and put the urn loudly onto the mantel,
pausing to work a knot from her throat. "Anyway, that's all
I feel compelled to say today. If you want to hear a different
story about my dad you should talk to his best friend . . ." She
put her hand to her brow, locating Rick where she'd left him
minutes earlier. "Rick LaForge, who works every day to make
Wicklow notable rather than notorious." She seemed on the
verge of laughing, but then her face turned grim. The crowd
had gone silent. An arm reached out, begging her off the ped-
estal. Glennis swiped it away.

"And if you want Rick to tell a *happy* story about my dad
then you might start the conversation by telling him 'thanks.'
Or better yet, tell him that you're sorry for thinking he could
ever have done something so terrible."

At this, she finally stepped down, floating through the
crowd and up the stairs. No one followed. If she had any
friends, none of them were there. It occurred to Rick, then,
that perhaps he was her only real friend, and that with Emmit
gone she may have been his. He wondered if it was up to
him to follow her upstairs, but he didn't do it. There was a
husband, after all, whose parents were in attendance. So he
stayed downstairs, doing just what she'd suggested. He told the
story about his last-second throw in the state quarterfinals and
Emmit's miraculous catch in the back of the end zone. And a
dozen other anecdotes about his friend, and about Janice too,
stories of when the quarry was still getting deeper and the mill
still smoked, stories whose backdrops were the happier, healthier settings of Wicklow before the rust.

RELEASE PARTY

Usually, Billy Nolan dreams of clouds—lacy strands of cirrus, big puffy cumulus. His unconscious self likes to go fishing or camping, and always, featured prominently in these dreamscapes, are clouds. A palm reader he dated some years ago said this meant he had a buoyant, youthful soul. Though later on, as she threw his clothing out the window of her apartment, she'd called him an overgrown child.

But on this morning, he wakes from a dream of undead teenagers being hunted by a maniac in a pickup truck. The details are fading now, but the sense of menace is difficult to shake off.

As he sits up in the backseat of his Dodge and rubs sleep from his eyes, he remembers that his son is being released from prison today, so the nightmare may only be a manifestation of this day's pressures. Except that Billy Nolan doesn't feel stress. That people worry over things not immediately in front of them mystifies him. His ex-wife, before she found him "emotionally detached," had seemed to admire his unflappability. But as the marriage soured, Kate came to view it as the primary symptom of what she called his "enduring adolescence."

In the wake of the palm reader breakup, it occurred to him that, for all their efforts, the women in his life were failing to fix him. So he decided to do it himself. He quit smoking and drinking, and gave the money he'd have spent each week on those things to an investment guru who held meetings in a karate studio in Ukrainian Village. Sensei Gary preached the power of chanting to force a better reality. *There's a rich man inside you,* everyone recited at the start of meetings, *just let him out. The flood is coming, be inflatable.* Gary wore long hair and a well-groomed beard. His palms bore scars from catching throwing stars, which he'd rub while recounting karate stories with biblical self-help morals attached. *Look beyond your clenched fists, and you'll begin to see the signs from God.*

Billy doesn't believe in God any more than he believes in stress, but he did like going to a place with swords on the walls, and the time spent with Sensei Gary had been reaping real benefits. He'd begun working out again and joined a softball league. He was holding down a job and even started sending postcards to his son again. But then the FBI crashed the dojo and led kimono Jesus out in handcuffs. When it all got sorted out months later, the money everyone had been tithing in got redistributed, and Billy concluded that having all that liquor and tobacco cash come rushing back to him was its own sign from God.

As Billy rubs his forehead, the hangover pulses beneath his fingers. He tries to think, but there are no chants to negate a night of heavy drinking. When his eyes finally refocus, the day outside his car is bright, the sun already high. A flyer pinned beneath his windshield wiper flutters in the breeze, and beyond it, the bar at which he spent the previous evening sits up against the sidewalk, its neon light turned off, a big silver padlock on the door. Across the street, the open pastures of a cemetery roll away toward a distant wood of low-hanging willows. Among the headstones are dozens of tree stumps lopped at waist height, and a smattering of newly planted trees with nylon bags slung around their bases.

Billy slides across the backseat and gets out to retrieve the paper tucked beneath his wiper blade. *Dear Asshole,* it reads. *I took your keys. If you want them back the bar opens again at 4 p.m.—Armstrong*

When he lowers the paper, he notices half a face looking out at him from the front passenger seat of his car, the top of a head and eyes. The rest of what appears to be a teenage girl cowers in the well beneath the dashboard. He walks around the car and opens the passenger door.

"What are you supposed to be?" he asks.

The teenager presses herself sheepishly up onto the seat. She wears dark cargo pants and a black tank top. Her bare shoulders and arms swirl with tattoos of spiderwebs and cat's-eyes. Her black hair and combat boots shine, but the rest of her is grungy and tattered.

"Did I dream of you?" he asks. "Are you from my dreams?"

She rolls her eyes. "Ew, sick, don't get all pervy."

"Hold on, I'm still waking up here. I was asleep in the back—" He yanks the door open wider. "This is *my* car, you know."

She looks cautiously up the street, one way then the other. She's nearly pretty, but in a way he finds unfortunate, as if she's been crying all week, or has chosen a style of eye shadow that means to give that impression.

"*You* let me in," she says. "That freak was chasing us."

"What freak?"

"The guy in the green truck."

"I thought I dreamed that too."

"Yeah, you were pretty out of it when I knocked on the window. Then you went right back to sleep. You're a really loud snorer." The girl takes the note from his hand, reads it. "Well that sucks."

At the end of the block, the green pickup appears. The one from his dream or the one from the girl's account. Both. The truck idles a moment longer at the empty intersection, then turns and rumbles closer, the driver's head swinging from the cemetery on one side of the road to the empty storefronts on the other. The girl crawls back under the dash. The truck crunches through the gravel. Billy turns, staring directly at the approaching vehicle. The pickup stops abruptly, waits, then U-turns and disappears again down the empty block.

"Thanks," the girl says, climbing out again. "He's been circling the block forever. I wasn't even doing anything wrong. Isn't a cemetery like public property?"

"I don't think so," he says. "You got a vehicle around here?"

The girl motions to a small blue car parked several hundred yards down the street. "Do you think it's safe to make a run for it yet?"

"Tell you what . . ." Billy says, crumpling the note and dropping it on the ground. "Since I've apparently done you a great favor here, how about we make a run for it together, and then you give me a ride to someplace I can get some pancakes."

As they ride in her car through a tired-looking neighborhood, Billy thinks of Hartley's father-in-law, who once owned a home somewhere nearby. He recalls standing on its front lawn with his son a decade earlier, both of them in tuxedos waiting for a car to take them to the church.

He'd meant to visit his son in prison, but the eight-year sentence offered such a broad window. When Kate called last month to remind him of Hartley's early release, she described her disappointment at Billy not having made the trip to Grassland. But Billy refused her scorn, noting instead his surprise at the time having passed so suddenly.

"Parole?" he'd exclaimed. "Already?" Though by the end of their conversation his ex-wife made it clear that the time had probably not passed as easily for Hartley.

"I'm not a robot, Kate," he'd barked into the phone. "I get that this is important."

"You keep saying 'it's important,'" she said. "But you haven't said you'll be there when he gets out." This was Kate, always trying to cut through the trifling nature of conversation to get a person to make promises. "Billy," she said forcefully, "Hartley expects you to be there."

And so, as the satanic-looking girl drives him through Wicklow, he remarks at one house and another, wondering aloud whether it's the one he remembers standing in front of, ". . . which my son's father-in-law owned, and which my daughter-in-law then inherited, and now, shit, I think the bank seized it or something. I don't know. It's been hard times for them since Hartley went in."

"Went in where?" the girl asks. With each bump in the road the inky creatures on her arms shudder to life, and a measure of real fear stabs into his chest. He understands that undead teenagers aren't real, but he can't shake the sense that his dream has returned to muddle the reality of waking day.

When all the cigarette and booze money came back to him after the feds took down Sensei Gary, he'd gotten into more expensive habits, into pills especially, painkillers and ecstasy and some rarer pharmaceuticals trafficked in from Eastern European countries he'd never even heard of. He couldn't now reconcile this decision, but at the time an escalation had felt necessary. At his worst, he'd ended up in a pop-up camper in the North Woods of Wisconsin with someone's cleaning lady and a grocery bag loose with Slavic drugs. It was a mint-green pill he'd found tucked in the bag's paper seam that took him for a ride from which he still hadn't fully returned. The hallucinations dissipated in a day and a half, and the flashbacks quit after a week, but he continues experiencing episodes at least once a day when he abruptly loses confidence in the reality of what he's seeing. And as he stares at the dead-looking girl, one of these spells takes hold of him.

This is real, he chants in his head, but she is not a zombie. The zombies were just a dream. This is real, and yet you do not need to be concerned.

"So," the girl says, "where did your son go into?"

"Prison."

Her foot releases the accelerator. "I could tell something was bothering you."

"I'm pretty hungover."

She turns a corner around a used-car lot. A sign with a woodpecker on it announces WOODY'S HOT RODS, but the cars behind the fence all look broken down. A minute later she's pulling over in front of a diner.

"This place used to be an abortion clinic," she says. "So I wouldn't eat the eggs." She blinks, waiting. "Before that it was a diner. Again. But before." When he still doesn't get out of the car, she says, "Prison? Really?"

"But Hartley's actually a good kid."

"What'd he do?"

"He was a trader," Billy says. "In Chicago."

"I mean to get himself in prison. Did he kill someone or something?"

"He didn't mean to."

The girl nods. "Sure, just like the Soyfield Strangler."

He checks the time on his phone. "Who the hell's the Soyfield Strangler?"

"He was our local serial killer," she says, with pride. "Before they executed him, he gave an interview where he swore it wasn't his fault. He said he murdered all those people while he was *sleepwalking*." She pauses, wide-eyed, letting this information sink in.

Billy tries to be interested, but he can't look away from her tattoos. There's a quickening in his veins. A bitterness pools beneath his tongue. The mint-green pill is stalking him.

"And at the end of this interview," she continues, "they asked him what it was he'd been dreaming about *while* he was killing all those people, and do you know what he said?"

"Zombies?"

The girl bursts into laughter, then she laughs some more, taking quite a while to collect herself. "Not zombies, no," she finally says.

"What was it then?" Billy asks. "Oh shit, was it clouds?"

She laughs even harder, putting a finger up to beg his patience. Billy would mind this more were it not breaking up her air of undead menace, and the longer she goes on the more his heart settles into its usual rhythm.

"*So . . .*" he says. "What was it?"

The girl takes a deep restorative breath. "Never mind."

The windows of the abortion clinic bustle with hungry citizens, but Billy's own appetite has abandoned him, and it's getting close to time anyway. "It turns out I don't have time for pancakes," he announces, squinting past the diner at the dark ribbon of storm clouds on the horizon. "What I really need is a ride to the prison." He turns to the girl, staring into the caverns of her eyes. "I'll buy you some beer of course," he adds. "For your time, and trouble. But really, you'd be doing a tremendous thing for Hartley."

//

The year before, an investigator for the Illinois Department of Corrections came to Billy's apartment to ask whether he'd been planning to break his son out of jail. An unsigned letter had apparently been sent to the prison, addressed to Hartley, outlining just such a scheme. By the time the investigator had tracked Billy down they were ready to call it a hoax, though some trouble it caused anyway had earned Hartley a one-day extension of his sentence.

Thinking of it now, as the girl pulls into the quickie mart parking lot, Billy entertains the fantasy that maybe he *had* penned that letter, perhaps during his pharmaceutical bender. Maybe there's still time, he thinks. Still almost twenty minutes left to do what he should have done years ago, break his boy out.

When the girl has finally picked something out, the man at the register shakes his head. "Can't sell liquor for another fifteen minutes," he explains. "Blue laws."

"In another fifteen minutes," Billy says, "I have to be at Grassland. My son's getting out after four years and all he wants in the world is this beer." He sets his hand on the box the girl has chosen, a twelve-pack of wine coolers with tanned beachgoers lazing all over the packaging.

The clerk glances up at the security camera trained on his position. "Come back at five till and I'll see what I can do."

Outside the quickie mart, Billy and the girl stand looking at a billboard advertising a paintball arena called Derelict Mill DeadZone beside an older billboard for something called Trailer Park Meltdown.

"So paintball's pretty big around here?"

The girl shrugs. "This one guy is just buying up all the abandoned stuff around town and calling it postapocalyptic." She checks her phone and sighs. She says, "Look, I'm not going to be able to wait around at the prison. This is a one-way trip, okay?"

"You never told me," says Billy. "What does the Soyfield Strangler dream of?"

But then the door bucks open and the clerk waves them in. The ensuing transaction takes on the air of a drug deal. When it's finally over, Billy's phone reads two minutes before the hour.

//

There's an accident on the state highway. A jackknifed dairy tanker. A detour through cornfields. When they finally get to the prison there aren't any cars in the lot and Billy knows he's screwed before the guard opens his mouth.

"Already been released," the guard explains. "Gone home."

Billy dials Kate, but it goes to voice mail after one ring. "She's ignoring me, can you believe that?"

The girl's face appears to believe it just fine.

"All right," Billy says. "Just take me back to my car." He calls Kate again, straight to voice mail. "Kate, it's Billy, I don't know what happened. Okay, I fucked up, but there was this complete asswipe who stole my keys and I had to hitch my way to the prison, and now, I don't know, looks like they let Hartley out early? Anyway, call me. Are we doing a dinner or something? Tell Hartley congrats and I'll meet you guys wherever."

When he gets out beside his own car the girl speeds off down the sleepy gravel street. The dust cloud in her wake drifts over the cemetery. Above it, the band of darkness on the horizon has grown wider, dimly greenish, while the sun directly overhead drills down upon him.

It's even hotter in the car, and he can't roll the windows down. He checks his phone again, then goes to the door of the bar and kicks the padlock until dents appear in the wood behind the lock. Then he finds a hunk of cement and stands looking at himself in the bar's single window, trying to come to terms with the fact that breaking the glass will mean destroying the neon Chicago Bears sign behind it. Then his cell phone buzzes.

"Kate, I've been calling and calling—"

"Billy, listen to me."

"This complete cocksucker took my—"

"Billy."

"Uh-huh."

"We're being followed," Kate says. "By a crazy person. A man in a car has been following us since the prison and I think he wants to hurt Hartley. We've been driving in circles for half an hour and Hartley won't let me call the police."

"Where are you?" Billy asks.

"In Wicklow. Can you do something about this?"

"Hartley's right," Billy says. "No cops. Cops are worthless at a time like—"

"Billy . . ."

"Bring him to me."

"Who?"

"The crazy guy," Billy says. "I'm parked on the north side of the cemetery in Wicklow, just glide past me and, I don't know, I'll do something."

"This is insane, Billy. I'm calling the police. Neelish says this isn't up to us. He says I should call the police."

"That doesn't sound very entrepreneurial."

"I'm calling the police. We haven't done anything wrong." Other voices in her car rise up and then the call ends.

Billy carries the hunk of cement over to his Dodge. He sits on the fender. His phone vibrates again.

"Okay," says Kate. "I'm saying okay."

"All you've got to do is cruise past my car and I'll . . ." Billy pauses to think what he'll actually do. "I'll interrupt the pursuit."

Kate sighs. "Glennis says we're two minutes away. Are you ready for this?"

"I was born ready, Kate."

"Billy . . ."

"I'm ready, I'm ready."

"Do you have a plan?"

"Just cruise by." He weighs the football-size hunk of cement in his hand, crouches behind the front end of his car. The street is quiet. There aren't even any birds chirping. He listens to Kate explain to the others in the car that he has some sort of plan. There's commentary in the background from Hartley's stepfather that Billy can't quite make out beyond the man's doubtful tone. Then he hears Hartley murmuring assurances. Then Glennis's voice says, "Okay, okay, turn right here. Turn left I mean, oh Jesus—" Billy pockets his phone. He hears the engines approaching. His mind clears. He eyes the distant storm clouds. The flood is coming, he thinks, be unflappable. The seconds drag. A tendon winds tight inside his throwing shoulder. Kate's white Camry pulls past. Familiar faces blur by—the Indian man in shotgun, Hartley's calm blue eyes in the backseat. Then he sees the gray compact following behind. He lunges forward and heaves the cement. Glare obscures the windshield of the little car, until, in the last half moment before impact, the leafy shadow of an overhanging branch reveals an aged, wide-eyed face behind the wheel.

The windshield spiderwebs, caves inward. The car careens, losing speed, drifting slowly up onto the parkway along the cemetery's fence, until it sits at idle.

Billy stands in the road, his heart drumming his ribs. Kate's car taps the brakes at the end of the block, then banks hard, peeling out of sight. In the foreground, the wounded vehicle whines and sputters, but the driver's silhouette doesn't move. Slowly Billy approaches, popping the passenger door to find an old man behind the wheel, gasping shallowly.

"You okay, buddy?"

The man gives a faint headshake.

Billy snatches a small handgun off the passenger seat and pockets it. Beneath where the gun had lain, he discovers a slip of paper on which his son's name has been scrawled.

"What's this about, old-timer?"

The man's mouth levers open, but no words come out.

Billy's phone vibrates. Kate. He silences it. He holds the

paper in front of the man's eyes. "This is my son, you shit-head."

The old man's tongue moves up and down, the back of his throat flexes soundlessly. "It's coming," he finally rasps. "The dream again."

Billy's cell buzzes again. "What is it, Kate?"

"What *hap*pened?" she gasps.

"I've remedied the situation. Tell Hartley everything's taken care of." Billy pauses so that Kate can report his heroics. Overhead, the dark portion of the sky has grown considerably.

"Billy," Kate pleads, "what is *happening?*"

He leans back into the car to watch the old man suffer for breath. "I'm not entirely sure yet. I've thwarted a plot of some kind. But really, I think it's best if none of you knows any specifics."

"Billy . . ."

"You guys go out to dinner or whatever and I'll check in later." He ends the call, then gets into the passenger seat and closes the door. The car smells like burned oil. From a piece of newsprint on the floor, the skeletal face of Abe Lincoln gazes out of a cornfield. The old man lays his head against the window, his chest pulsing weakly. Billy pats down the man's clothes. There's no wallet or phone, only a clutch of casino chips in each pocket, which he digs out two and three at a time. The glossy gray markers look real enough, but when they're all lined up on Billy's thighs—eight thousand dollars' worth—he begins to doubt. Not since getting all that cash back from the Sensei Gary debacle has he held so much money at once.

"You don't look so lucky to me," Billy says.

The old man's eyes loll. His head tips forward and saliva runs down his chin.

Billy stuffs everything into his own pockets, puts his foot down into the well below the steering column, and presses the accelerator, reaching across to steer the car down the parkway and through the cemetery's open utility gate. The gravel road crackles as he winds deeper into the burial grounds, eventually cutting across a meadow of small flat plaques and into a stand of low-hanging willows that shield the car from the road.

"Hey old-timer, what was it you were saying before, about dreams coming again?" He clutches the old man's chin, tipping the head up. As he does this, a small metal hoop slides out of the man's mouth and lands on his shirt pocket. When Billy dries it off there's a slim gold wedding ring pinched in his fingers.

He turns off the car and gets out, walking back through the low-slung willow reeds. He scans the empty cemetery. Overhead, the gray-green trouble devours more and more of the sky, the temperature dropping as the light runs off, the air filling with electricity. The world in every direction is void of people. It feels, he thinks, like he's reentering his nightmare. The darkness will descend soon. The living dead will be along any minute now.

Billy walks a loop around the cemetery, looking for someone—a mourner, a cemetery employee, anyone to interrupt the eerie vacancy. He sits on a headstone and smokes his last four cigarettes in an unbroken chain. He tries to think.

Back at the gray car, he taps the window where the old man's scalp smudges the glass. "You're fucking with my head, grandpa." He raps the gun against the window. "I can see you breathing in there, motherfucker." He knows he's being cruel, but this still feels like part of his heroic performance. He imagines himself recalling these events later to the family he's saved. *His* family. Even the boy's stepfather will be rapt by the first-person account of such daring and sacrifice.

When his phone vibrates again he skips formalities and goes right into a description of the progress being made. "My investigation is nearly complete," he says. "I think I've gotten to the bottom of this bag."

"Bag?" Kate asks. "What bag?"

"I've been working on this case since last night, it turns out. I've been dreaming the facts. There's a satanic element to it, I think, and this Strangler person may also be connected somehow."

"Billy, are you drunk?"

"I've been trying to chant my way through this, Kate, to see the signs from God and all. But it's simpler than that. It has to be."

Kate doesn't understand what he's getting at. She passes the phone to their son.

"Hartley, tell your mother she may have been right about me." Billy yanks the driver's-side door open and watches the old man tumble to the ground. The fall is very convincing. "It turns out I'm not unflappable. My emotions may be detached after all."

He ends the call. The dark half of the sky churns wildly now. The wind makes chaos of the reedy strands of the willow tree. He unbuttons the old man's shirt, pulling it down his arms, twisting the fabric around the bony wrists, before shutting the shirt's hem up into the car door. Leaving the man in the dirt with his hands bound behind his back, Billy walks across the cemetery, climbing over the now-locked gate, across the street to where the bouncer sweeps the curb in front of the bar.

"You Armstrong?" Billy asks.

"And you're the pecker who loses all his charm after ten beers."

"Where the fuck are my keys, Armstrong?"

The bouncer thumbs over his shoulder.

Inside, it's empty and wet and everything smells like the mop. The bartender sees him coming and drops the keys loudly onto the bar top. Billy orders a beer.

"We're not doing this again," the bartender says.

Thunder rolls across the county. It begins to pour. Billy looks over his shoulder to watch the bouncer duck inside. The wind holds the door open against its hinges. A garbage can rolls down the street.

"Only one beer," Billy promises, trying to soften his voice. "I just need a minute here to figure out what exactly is going *on*." He takes the ring from his pocket. Watching the delicate gold hoop turn and shine calms him, transports him momentarily back into his own long-lost marriage. When he looks up again, the bartender is still wearing his doubtful face.

"Look," Billy says, trying for humor now, "my wife already thinks I'm drunk, so this is actually an attempt to meet expectations."

The bartender pushes the keys closer. "As I understand it, the ring is supposed to stay on the lady's finger."

//

At the bar's one window, with the bouncer eyeing him, Billy stares out into the storm's madness. Thunder shakes the building. The lights flicker. He feels it clench more tightly around him, the curse of the mint-green pill. He nudges the door open and the wind rips it wide. The sky is dark now. Lightning in all directions. A large piece of the tree across the street has fallen down and mangled the cemetery's iron fence. A dumpster lies on its side in the middle of the street. The long white body of a dead swan turns circles on the pavement like the hand of a clock. When he steps out into the sideways rain he can feel that there's ice involved, sticks, pebbles.

Back inside his car, he digs sleet from his ear. The windows are a whiteout. The weather and the hallucinations merge into a diverse mania—satanists and serial killers encircle the car, howling and scratching, angry girlfriends, bouncers. The scrambled din of all Sensei Gary's chants roils inside his head at once. He pulls the ring out again, pinching its narrow band, not unlike the one he once gave Kate. Later, of course, she gave it back. He'd refused, but she'd insisted. He didn't understand what she was getting at. Mr. Gupta, it turned out, was making it official. The day of the wedding, he took the ring down to Mel's and pawned it for cash. A decent return, he'd thought at the time, though later a vague remorse surfaced. A shadow of stress perhaps. But as he holds it now he feels a small measure of hope that the precious things he's forfeited in life might someday return.

The dead swan slaps the windshield, its pus-yellow eyes like tentacle suckers on the glass, dragging him to the bottom of the new sea beneath Sensei Gary's great flood. But then the storm's madness begins to back off. First the wind, then the raindrops clarify to individual strikes on the car's roof, until there's almost no sound at all. The windows clear, a smooth black sky coming on behind the departing tempest, stars poking through, a moon rising.

When he can no longer hear thunder, he gets out and crosses the section of fence taken down by the fallen tree, hurrying toward the old man, finding him exactly where he'd fallen, soaked and mud-splattered. Billy lifts him back into the driver's seat of the gray compact, pulls the shirt back over his bony shoulders.

"Okay," he tells the man. "I get it. You're all messed up. I can see that. I'm sorry. But I'm just not sure how I was supposed to have played this."

One side of the aged face is sunken and lifeless while the other jumps with seizures. A scallop of mud hangs in the hairline.

Billy picks willow reeds off the man's cheek. "Was this some kind of vengeance operation?" He searches the darkness for the neon bar light at the far edge of the cemetery, but the power is out everywhere. He pats his shirt pocket, but his cigarettes are gone. It occurs to him that maybe this is exactly what stress feels like. A doubt in one's prospects? A sense that recent behavior will not be received well when discovered by others? Certainly a crime has been committed, with a deadly hunk of cement. And he supposes additional charges may be in order for having held the man for so many hours, for having called this elderly gentleman "shithead" and "motherfucker."

"Was it the lady my son hit with his car? Was she someone to you?" Billy touches the man's shoulder, he rebuttons the shirt, fixes the collar. He's using his kindest tone now. He only means to talk with the old man, one last conversation, to let him speak his piece before the end. "Okay, yes, that was an awful thing Hartley did, getting into that car. But you don't know my son. Hartley's a good man, a forgiving man."

Billy thinks of the one letter he got from Hartley, post-marked from Grassland. In this note, the boy had described his concerns about Sensei Gary. He'd been pleased to hear his father was living a healthier life, but he'd asked some very simple questions about the guru, which, by the time the letter had reached Billy, were proving prophetic. And at the end, Hartley added a postscript explaining that if forgiveness meant something in the course of his father's self-improvement then Billy was indeed forgiven, and that on some primal level it had actually pleased Hartley to know his father cared enough to want to break him out of jail.

"Forgiveness!" Billy exclaims, swiping the old man gently on the shoulder. "For a crime I didn't even commit!"

Then his phone vibrates again. Kate and her questions. Ignore.

The moon rises higher and the car grows cold. Billy tells the old man stories about Hartley as a boy—naïve but loyal, savvy with a dollar, good to his mother. His phone buzzes again and again. Hartley, then Kate, then Hartley. The day's voice mails, when he listens to them all in a row, tell a dramatic narrative. At first there's much excitement over a man who's thrown a rock at a car, then warnings of a terrible storm. The most recent message offers an address where Billy might seek refuge with his family until the highways are navigable. But he isn't looking for refuge, and he doesn't want to talk to anyone except the old man.

Headlights appear in the distance. He thinks it's bar traffic at first, but when he retrieves his bearings he realizes it's someone driving one of the cemetery's winding inner roads, ranging closer then farther, a single bifocal light source in the power outage.

Then the headlights turn and sweep and the willow tree's stringy wet branches explode with light. Billy's heart thrashes inside his rib cage. The lights mercifully curve away. The tree darkens. When his eyes recalibrate, the truck is closer than he realized, only a few hundred feet away now, moving left to right. It's the green truck from his dream. He thinks of the young satanist in his car that morning, an undead girl with living monsters on her flesh. In this way, reality feels irretrievably lost. Everything forfeited to false and damaged memory. He lays his palms on his thighs, feels the wedding ring nestled beside the pistol, the clutch of casino chips. There's a rich man inside you, he tells himself. You have a wife and family and everything lost can still be recovered.

The truck makes another U-turn, the tree illuminating then extinguishing. The pickup bumps past at only fifty feet now. Behind it, the moonlight sparkles on a cloud of yellow gas. The mist billows toward him, pushing in among the low-slung branches, until the car is engulfed, the world beyond a muffled ghost. It's coming, he thinks, the dream again. This is the part when everything gives way to clouds.

He turns to his companion, wanting just one answer. "Hey, come on, are you seeing this?" He jostles the old man's shoulder. "Hey, old-timer, come on, I got a question for you." He touches the man's face, wipes the mud off his brow, sweeps the hair to a tidier angle. "Hey, come on, seriously, you hearing me?" But the old man doesn't move, not even to breathe. Billy runs his fingers down to the man's neck. He waits and waits. He thinks of the letter he might've written. He knows he didn't write it, but he wishes he had. He wishes he'd broken Hartley out of jail, or at least been there today to welcome him free. Some days he fears what he's capable of, others what he's not.

"Hey," he whispers, giving up on the search for a pulse. "Hey, old-timer, come on now, just tell me this one thing, I gotta know, please." He waits for a sign of life, a sign of God, anything. Outside, the world is powerless and he's floating through dreams inside a golden cloud. "Old man," he whispers, "tell me, please, I gotta know, seriously, what does the Soyfield Strangler dream of?"

WE'VE LOST OUR PLACE

One entire wall of the psychiatrist's office is lined with self-help books. Bright softcover tomes that betray the doctor's otherwise stuffy academic style, lend the space, from the right vantage point, the feel of a child's room, gaudy with cheer. On some of the shelves are gaps in the books where little hand puzzles and squeeze balls sit, as well as a big red clock that has never, in three-and-a-half years, been off by so much as one minute.

Victor glares at the minute hand, waiting for it to jump. Time has a tendency to leap on him these days, sneaking past when he isn't looking. "I just wish," he says, "that I could recall coming *back* to life. I remember heading for the guardrail, but then nothing else for days afterward, weeks really. No memory at all of my recovery. Doesn't that seem odd to you?"

Dr. Simmons rubs his eyes, stealing his own glance at the red clock. "Victor, don't you think our time would be better spent discussing the fact that Hartley Nolan went free today?"

"I thought he got out yesterday."

The psychiatrist shrugs. "Either way . . ."

Victor looks out the window now, at a dimming green sky. "Yeah, but is there a name for what I'm describing? For feeling like maybe I *didn't* survive?"

"This is the kind of thing you should put into your next catharsis letter. So we can discuss it some other time."

Dr. Simmons and his letters. They are, as far as Victor can tell, just a way for the psychiatrist to put off topics he doesn't care to explore. Just a way to keep Victor occupied in the middle of nights rather than having the doctor paged. Occasionally, when a session gets slow, Simmons will open one—a note to Victor's in-laws, to his dead mother, to the killer even—and read it aloud so that Victor can revisit his feelings of rage and disaster in the blunt light of day.

At one time, years ago, they were sort of friends, the psychiatrist and Victor. Or, not friends, exactly, but the kind of men who could stand beside one another at a barbecue talking while their wives genuinely enjoyed each other's company nearby. Victor pauses to try to remember it, to carefully reconstruct in his mind the particular sound of Sonia's laughter carrying across someone's backyard. There was an above-ground pool in the background, full of shiny fat children, oppressive heat, mosquitoes. But whenever he'd been struck by the sense that he couldn't stand being there another minute, Sonia's laughter would travel across the yard and he'd be fortified with some spare measure of her patience and good cheer. But this was a long time ago, before everything, back when Lawrence Simmons was just some dope at a barbecue and Victor wasn't anyone's charity case.

"But there's got to be a name for this feeling," Victor persists. "Right?"

"Cotard's syndrome," Dr. Simmons says without much conviction. "It's a delusion that one is actually deceased."

"Cotard's syndrome," Victor recites as though it is the long-awaited answer to a trivia question. "Do you think that's what my problem is?"

"Do you mean being delusional or actually being dead?" Simmons takes his own glance at the churning sky outside his office. "Your problem, Victor, is that you have depression. You never even began to cope with Sonia's death. And on top of that, now you have some memory loss connected to a more recent trauma, which is actually quite normal. Tell me, when does your memory pick up again? After what you did?"

Victor remembers losing control, going toward the cliff, then nothing for weeks after until he recalls being shown a newspaper article with a photo of his truck hanging over the edge of the quarry, the guardrail tangled in the rear axle. The time between is a blank. The whole supposed recovery. A blur of pain and confusion, black eyes and broken ribs, a freckle of a scar where the IV had anchored, a hospital bracelet supposing he'd healed. Then home again, under orders to rest, while people appeared at his door with food. June brought meatballs. A neighbor brought lasagna. An elderly woman whose husband was buried in Oak Hill brought a different kind of lasagna. Those early days of being back home weren't unlike after Sonia died. Nights of gifted food from plastic containers he'd have to wash and return. Or just throw away, which he may have done. He can't remember that either. But memory appears to be losing its value anyway with life on repeat. Tragedy followed by Italian food. One day, he was just back in his daily existence again—eating meals, taking showers, going to work, three months now since running himself off the road—but all of it, every second of his

life lately, is attended by the unwavering sense that he didn't actually survive, that his ongoing experience of the present is just
a flight of the mind conjured in the last moment before death.

"God, Vic, that's some pretty grim material." June was
standing in the doorway of his office, her hands conspicuously
clutching a tri-folded piece of paper. It was his first day back
at Oak Hill. "Well, I'm here listening to you," she continued,
"so I'm pretty sure you're alive."

Victor went on to explain that her meatball tray had been
thrown out by the cleaning lady.

June didn't mind. She had others like it. And she had other
things to discuss.

"So do I," he said, his attention drifting out his office window. "Tell me, where have all my oak trees gone?"

She'd had them all cut down while he was in the hospital.
A clean break, she was calling it. New trees. New life. New
everything. "Now you just need to sell this place and start
over. Somewhere else."

"My wife's buried here."

"And you can visit her anytime," June said. "Like a normal
person."

He continued to gaze out at the culled plain of Oak Hill.
Only the evergreens and willows remained, the mausoleums
overlarge and menacing in the open air. "But they were *my*
trees," he lamented. "I would've liked to have said good-bye
first."

"It doesn't work that way," June said. "And you weren't
going to take care of it yourself." She handed him the folded
paper, typewritten with her name signed at the bottom. "You've
become totally . . ." She searched for a word, then discarded it.
"Do you know what the new girl calls you?"

"The one who's always taking things off my desk? Didn't I fire her?"

"No," said June. "You've been *threatening* to fire her, for months. That's my point. You've become completely inert. You're here right now, but you're not really *here*. Do you understand what I'm saying, Victor?"

He tried to place himself in time. He could have sworn he'd fired this person. In the near future she was sure to be fired. "Who even found that girl? Is Gunner hiring people?"

June motioned to the paper she'd handed him. "That's my two weeks' notice, Victor. Gunner's leaving too. I know this place is special to you, but I really don't think you should work here anymore either."

He turned back to the window, the fresh-cut stumps like so many new markers, the dead suddenly piling up around him. He blinked and the cemetery disappeared. A storm now complicates the sky outside the psychiatrist's office. "June's been gone two months now," Victor explains, "and I still haven't fired the new girl."

Dr. Simmons reclines at hearing this, touches his chin. "So, what was she calling you?"

Victor's attention comes slowly back into the room. "Who?"

"The new girl."

"She isn't even that new anymore," Victor says. "But I can't remember her name. I don't think I ever learned it."

"But what was she calling you?"

Victor finally puts his full attention on Simmons. "Dead man walking."

The doctor stands up and moves to the bookshelves. He plucks a small pink stress ball off one shelf. A book titled *So You're Grieving, Now What?* tilts into the vacated space. "Well,

I suppose that explains your bout of Cotard's syndrome," he says. "But what do you think of June's suggestion to sell the cemetery?" He turns and holds his eyes on Victor, strokes his beard. "Or, what do you imagine *Sonia* would think about it?"

"I don't know."

"You don't know?"

Victor looks at the clock again. "It takes a lot of effort to recall my old life anymore. Mostly I just keep revisiting the crappiest parts of this years-long aftermath."

Simmons sits down again. "Sounds more like post-traumatic stress to me."

Victor stares at the minute hand. It seems poised to swing forward at any moment. "Actually, Sonia thought it was a little odd that a person could even own a cemetery to begin with. She thought it was one of my personality quirks, a need to possess meaningful things. Or control them. I can't recall exactly how she put it."

"Try to recall," Simmons insists.

"She wasn't being mean or anything. She was never mean, ever. She was very funny, actually, around me. With everyone else she was so completely cool all the time. I mean 'cool,' as in everybody thought she was cool, but also . . . cold."

"She was *cold*?"

Victor gets up and moves to the wall of books, taking down *So You're Grieving, Now What?* "With her parents, I mean. But they were the cold ones, really. There was always a disconnect between them, or something." He dumps the book back on the shelf, then turns to face Simmons. "But with me, she was never cold. With me, she had this goofy sense of humor that no one else got to see, these lame jokes."

"I had no idea," the psychiatrist says.

"Sometimes, she'd take off her wedding ring and drop it in the loose change jar we kept on the counter, and say, 'Victor, I need change!'"

Simmons smirks painfully. The stress ball shrinks into his fist.

"Get it? I need change?" A smile tries to lift Victor's face, but then the nausea moves in, a kind of impending motion sickness, and he can feel it happening again, time spiriting past him.

This is how the days go missing. A series of small glitches in the continuum where memory fails to record. He'll lie down on his couch at work for a lunch-break nap only to rise in the middle of the night following, or he'll snap awake behind the wheel wondering how long he's been coasting unaware since leaving Dr. Simmons's office, inching back across Wicklow in his spray truck as a tempest rages all around. Rain and hail, the howl of tornado sirens. The whiteout against the windows is something he can't look away from, a thrilling natural static playing on all the screens of his life. This is how it felt as he'd hurtled toward that guardrail—fear giving way to wonder, all senses muted, body closed up inside the vessel that would take him to the other side.

Beyond the windshield squall, he can barely make out a green light ahead. It turns yellow, then red, then blinks red, then goes out. He idles at the center of town, waiting for instructions, for Sonia. He tries to conjure her in his mind, the deep green pools of her eyes, the crimp in her cheek as she'd deliver a corny joke. But then the static melts away and the world comes back into focus, revealing a dark and dripping night strewn with aftermath. Trees lie on top of fences and cars and garages. Power lines crackle on sidewalks. The road is scattered with branches and boards and lawn furniture.

He'd been with June a moment ago, he thinks, or was it Dr. Simmons? How is it that only Sonia feels distant from these landing points?

//

At Oak Hill the power is out, but the moonlight glows on the rain-dappled window of his office, and he can see June's resignation letter is still on his desk beside a pile of unsent bills. His employees have been afraid to mail anything since the new girl inadvertently put one of his catharsis letters in the outgoing mail last fall. Victor had actually wanted to send it, at first. He'd wanted to start some trouble for Hartley Nolan, get him beat up by the guards or thrown into a hole. But this, it turned out, was only drunken scheming. Just a man in a darkened cemetery building afraid to go back to his empty house. In the light of the next day, imagining how silly this plot would sound if read aloud by Dr. Simmons, he buried the letter in the files on his desk.

Thinking, now, of the nights he spends sleeping on his office couch, avoiding his widower's mattress, it occurs to him that he is here once again, alone and afraid. Then he feels time about to slip past him again, the way he gets up some mornings and another year has gone by without Sonia, the way a week in the hospital vanishes from memory, the way the oak slayers—still here a month ago, wondering, like him, where their beloved trees had gone—have suddenly now disappeared too.

"Where are you?" he says, the sound of his voice waking him into the reality that he is in his truck again, weaving across the cemetery grounds dragging behind him a cloud of poison. "What is the point of this anymore?"

Victor steps on the brake and the spray truck skids on the

wet turf. In the glow of his headlights the soaking willow trees glisten fantastically. The yellow cloud overtakes him from behind, an enveloping wave that churns in the high beams, blurring the view. But then, as the cloud settles into a dense blanket along the ground, he can see it clearly, a car beneath the tree ahead, a piece of cement lodged in the windshield.

Victor gets out, his long shadow staggering across the vehicle's hood. There are faces inside. One man appears to be in late middle age, the other much older. They stare numbly into the headlights.

Victor motions to the windshield. "Storm do that?"

The men don't move.

He skirts around the front bumper and raps his knuckle on the passenger door.

The man on the other side of the glass turns, rolls down the window, and asks in a quiet beseech, "Are you real?"

Victor squints deeper into the car. The elderly man behind the wheel doesn't move, but the face looks vaguely familiar. If he would say something, Victor thinks he could identify him. A regular visitor, perhaps. People come to the cemetery after hours all the time, and they aren't always teenagers. Honest mourners sneak in too. Their grief hits them in the middle of the night and they come quietly through the dark to visit a loved one.

"Cemetery's closed," Victor announces.

The middle-aged passenger digs into his eye sockets, then looks up again at Victor in disbelief.

"Is everything all right?" Victor asks.

"I see things," the man finally says, "that aren't always there."

Victor motions to the elderly driver. "Is *he* all right?"

The passenger shakes his head.

"Is he dead?"

"Uh-huh."

This happens too, now and again, people without the means to pay for services trying to bury a loved one after hours. It's never happened here before, but it does happen. The grief, as he understands it, makes them do things they shouldn't do.

"Sorry," Victor says. "But you can't just bury him yourself. There are laws. I'm gonna have to call the police."

"You're freaking me out," the man says. "Walking out of the fog like that, in a cemetery, at night."

"I own this place. You're trespassing."

"Isn't a cemetery like public property?"

Victor looks at the dead man's face again. "Was he your father or something?"

"No."

"He looks familiar."

"I wasn't trying to bury him."

"What were you trying to do then?"

The man shrugs. "I'm not exactly sure anymore. I was acting heroically, and then, I don't know, when it was over I started feeling less heroic about it."

"What I'd like to know," says Victor, "is why the dead guy's behind the wheel."

The passenger takes a breath and nods as if this is a question that he too has been wrestling with. He then seems to drift, momentarily lost in thought, before abruptly jerking his attention back into the present. "But you are *here* right now, right?"

Victor tries again to remember waking up in the hospital, tries to fill in the missing time. It seems important to recall his return to life to believe in it. But also, he needs to know how he felt about it at the time, to decide once and for all whether his fortunes have turned for better or worse. The before he remembers well enough—the weeks of debilitating panic, the relentless insomnia, the sharp turn beside the quarry—then what? Home again, with Italian food. A house call from Dr. Simmons.

"No charge," the psychiatrist had said in a magnanimous voice, pressing into Victor's living room and digging himself a seat among the piles of dirty laundry and dried-out food trays.

"I wasn't aware I'd been paying you in the first place," Victor replied.

"You haven't."

"Good, because it isn't working."

"Well, I'm not here as your therapist today anyway," said Simmons. "I'm taking off my doctor hat here. I'm speaking to you as a friend."

"I don't think we *are* friends."

"Maybe not, but I knew you back when Sonia was alive, and I've been meeting with you because I liked her. Everybody did." Simmons took a breath and looked at Victor with a face that seemed to wonder what a person like Sonia had ever seen in him. And then he spoke for a time on the merits of reaching rock bottom, all paths leading upward, and so on, until Victor had passed through feelings of annoyance and boredom to plain fatigue. And then Simmons realized he'd been droning on and he cleared his throat and said, again, "Look, Victor, my doctor hat's off now, okay?"

Victor slumped against the couch arm, but pain radiated through his rib cage, and he sat up straight. "What is it you're getting at, Larry?"

"Forgive me for bringing this up, but . . ." The doctor

trailed off again, sucking his teeth and looking around, inter-
rupting himself with tangential apologies and streams of psy-
chojargon, until finally he'd managed to ask if what his wife
had heard was true, that someone had stolen the wedding ring
off Sonia's finger during the wake.

Right out of the casket, Victor confirmed. His head shook
as he recounted it, the minor perversion of petty crime atop
such monstrous tragedy. It took him four days to realize the
simple opportunity he'd missed to make things right. But it
was his cemetery, wasn't it? So he rose from his office couch in
the middle of the night, pulled on his work boots, and under
cover of a thick yellow haze, he dug up the casket himself and
put his own ring inside with her.

That part of the story, Simmons admitted, he hadn't heard
before. And for the first time the doctor looked uncomfortable,
regretful, it seemed, that he'd asked. So it was Victor's turn to be
magnanimous, to mercifully change the subject. He said, trying
to conjure the best memory of all, "Did you know that Sonia and
I met for the first time *in* Oak Hill, *before* I bought the place?"

But Simmons wanted to hear more of the heavy stuff after
all. "So you saw her again, when you opened the casket," he
said. "You saw her one last time?"

Victor nodded, but he tried not to think of it. He sent his
mind chasing after any other memory, even those most grim
moments of static and doubt as the guardrail rushed toward him.

The psychiatrist leaned forward, resting his forearms on his
knees. He had his doctor hat back on, Victor could tell. He
said, "Do you wish you hadn't done it?"

Victor exhaled, wincing as his broken rib cage contracted.
He lifted his shirt to touch gently the most tender spot on the
left side. "What do you mean by 'it'?"

"We've lost our place, I think."

And Victor could feel himself slipping again, losing his place. A moment later, the psychiatrist was gone from the couch and the Tupperware went into the garbage and the oak trees fell and a look of sudden clarity washes over the face of the man inside the little gray car with the shattered windshield. "But it *is* a good idea," the man says. "Yeah. We *should* bury him."

Victor shakes his head. "I think we've lost our place."

"But it was your idea," the man says. "And we're already in a cemetery."

"You can't," Victor says. "It's against the law."

"I'll take the fall if someone finds out. It's the least I can do to give him a burial." The man gets out of the car. "How about this?" He digs a handful of casino chips out of his pocket and offers them. "There's four thousand dollars here. You help me put him in the ground and when it's done the cash is yours."

Victor looks at the gray chips on the man's palm, shining in the moonlight like oak slayers with their legs tucked under.

"It was the old guy's money," the man says. "He had a heart attack or something. Natural causes. So really he's just paying his own burial expenses."

Victor peers in at the dead man again. He knows him from somewhere, he's sure now. "This is absurd. This is not happening."

"That's what *I'm* afraid of. I honestly can't tell what's real anymore—"

"I mean *this* isn't happening," says Victor. "I'm not letting you illegally dump a body in my cemetery. It's time to call the police."

"I'll call them for you," the man says. "Someone's got to

sort this out." He leans back against the car door with his phone to his ear. He says, "Kate, how is everyone? Okay. Yeah, what a storm, huh? Yep. Well, listen, there's this guy who's stonewalling me here at the cemetery, with the body. Yeah, the body. The old guy didn't make it. But he went peacefully, so— Kate, come on, keep it together. You did the right thing calling me. He was seriously troubled, and now, well, he's gone to a better— Okay, yeah, I'm just calling to let you guys know I'm gonna be a while longer here. Honestly, I don't know if I'm gonna make it at all." He waits a moment, listening to the person on the other end of the line, or just trying to think of what else to say. Then he ends the call.

"I thought you were calling the cops," Victor asks.

"All the cops are gonna do is put the guy in an icebox until they find out he hasn't got a friend in the world. Look at him. He hasn't got any family. Trust me. He's no one. I can just tell." The man takes the casino chips out again, pours them from one hand into the other, his face like a game show host's. "Here, I'm adding two more grand. That's six thousand. A simple transaction. I've got a dead body, you've got a cemetery—"

"Maybe I'm selling the cemetery."

"Even better." The man steps closer, trying to press the chips into Victor's hand. It seems at any moment that black legs will emerge from beneath each one.

"And if the cops come asking about it," the man continues, "you can tell them you agreed to it under duress. You can tell them I threatened you." He digs into his pocket and presents a small handgun on his open palm. It looks like a toy, but Victor can tell it's real by the way it wears the moonlight.

"Fine, seven thousand," the man says. "It's practically

all I've got. I can't give you any more." He drops the first six thousand at Victor's feet, and jams his free hand into his pocket. His face is turning feverish, desperate. "What do you say? Let's put him in the ground so you can get home in time to kiss your kids good night."

"I don't have any kids."

"Your wife then."

"I'm calling the cops," says Victor.

In an instant, the gun disappears into the man's palm and a second later it's pointing between Victor's eyes, the coppery glint of the bullet winking from inside the barrel. He feels his heart pause and petrify, his last breath catching inside his chest. His senses dull and the static takes over. As if from a great distance, from the far side of the handgun, he hears the man's voice say, "I don't want to shoot you, but I will if I have to, if you can't be reasonable."

"Do it," Victor says. He can barely hear his own voice.

The man lowers the barrel to Victor's chest, presses it to his sternum.

Victor closes his eyes, his heart punching back against the gun.

"Eight thousand," the man says. His voice is small and tinny, a sound mostly caught in his throat, as if it is *his* chest at which a gun is pointed. "That's everything."

"No," Victor says. "Do it. Just go ahead."

With his free hand, the man digs into his pocket again, offers more chips. "That's everything, I swear. Don't be like this. It's a good deal. It's everything I've got." His face drips and shines, absurd and hysterical, this stranger with his little gun and his far-off voice, his pockets spilling with coins.

Victor thinks of the loose change jar on the counter at

home, the crimp in Sonia's cheek. He wants to laugh, but it isn't funny, this part of his life. What does it mean, he wonders, not to possess the memory of coming back from death? A return unwitnessed, unwanted. Just a man standing up again and moving toward his next end. These are the thoughts that wash through him as his life spools away. He's at the end again now. He knows it. His eyes sting, the static softens and thickens in his ears. A sucking void wells up at the center of his body, a warm stream running through his chest with a current that sweeps him into the past, waking him back into the precious few memories of his long-gone mother, onto spring-green ball fields of his youth, into laboratories full of discovery, and finally into the days of Sonia. She is alive again beside him on this river of time reclaimed. The two of them on a summer morning in bed with the sun coming up and the *flop* of the newspaper hitting the stoop, a chorus of songbirds not yet poisoned, a wife not yet lost, a whole town decaying but not yet dead. It is years ago now and Sonia's ring is still on her finger and the cemetery still has its trees, the adoption papers are in the spare bedroom and the future is a promise yet to be broken.

He can't even hear the shot, the static is so loud. The river of memories is a warm rushing wound at his core. Wet grass cradles the back of his head. Yellow haze swirls all around. Beyond the static, he can barely hear the shooter's voice begging forgiveness. There are sirens in the distance and then bright lights overhead. As he tries to paddle back into the days of Sonia, he can feel the tickle of forceps digging a gnarled metal tooth out of his chest. He can hear the bloody bullet hit the tray.

Then there's nothing. Just a long silent leap through darkness and void. A night without a moon, a ring sliding off his finger as the casket lid rose.

She looked small, he thought. She looked as the birds would later appear when the yellow mist brought them down from their trees, shrunken and slight, as if the poison had collapsed their hollow bones, as if they were becoming chicks again in death. Sonia, he'd thought, pressing the lid shut again, had looked like a child.

//

In a corner of this utter dark, a bulb of faintest light takes shape and warms, slicing sideways with a parting of lids. His vision returns. He's awake again in the recent past, returned to the moment right before the end. The man with the gun still stands before him, the bullet still in the chamber. The moon-lit world glistens everywhere, the rainwater like liquid gold clinging to the willow reeds and the grass and the casino chips.

"Wait," Victor says. "Where'd you get that?"

The man lowers the gun, relief ripping through his face. His nerve seems to shatter and melt. He looks in his other hand at the casino markers, at a slim gold ring half-hidden beneath one chip. "You mean the ring? I found it."

"Where?"

"On him." The man turns and motions to the gray car. "In his . . . pocket."

Victor turns too, and he can see now what he couldn't before. He opens the door and measures the aged face, touches the cold hands. He presses a finger under the jaw to make certain that Raymond Bello is dead. "You were right," he says. "This guy *is* nobody. He doesn't have any family." Victor puts his other hand to his own neck, feels for a pulse.

The man scrambles to pick up the other casino markers in

the wet grass, offering them all in a heaping two-handed bowl. "So?" he says. "Can we bury him then?"

Somewhere, hundreds of yards away, a transformer goes back online. Victor can hear the hum of the neighborhood refilling with electrons, and beneath his finger the beat of his own pulse. Distant streetlamps blink awake in a line leading straight out of town. In the new light, the moon's strange pall wilts from the man's face. His air of menace falls away and he seems suddenly chastened and meek. His hands, Victor realizes, are shaking, the gold hoop burrowing deeper into the chips. "So?" the stranger begs. "What do you think?"

Victor lifts the ring from the hoard of casino markers, examines it on his palm. "I need change," he whispers. He thinks of the first words he ever said to Sonia, and then he thinks of the last.

"Sorry," he says aloud, "but I don't work here anymore."

REMOVAL SERVICES

S onia thought of her try at college, a memory of two boys coaxing her into a fraternity house bedroom where they'd arranged some cocaine on a table in the shape of a cross. Her first and only time with the stuff, but she'd gone along with it. Later the boys' pants came off and she'd gone along with that too. The whole thing failed to bring her any regret the next day. Entire semesters passed without her imagining what her thirty-nine-year-old self might wake up remembering, but then Middle-Western flunked her out and she tired of her own promiscuity.

She started going to church again, to a sparsely attended weekday service down the road from campus, in Wicklow, presided over by a man who'd been dismissed from her parents' church in Tower Hill when Sonia was a girl. He'd been the youth minister back then. Kids liked him. Sonia liked him. He'd worn his hair shaggy, like Christ. In a private moment, he'd showed Sonia where he'd mutilated his palms as a teenager. "Stigmata," he'd claimed. But watching him murmur his way through those weekday services so many years later, she couldn't fall for him again, so she walked out of the church into a cemetery down the street.

She liked to stroll through Oak Hill from time to time. It needed visitors. It needed upkeep. She picked up windblown garbage as she went, moved aside branches when they'd fallen onto gravestones.

"Do you work here?" asked a voice.

Sonia spun around to find a man standing behind her. He looked slightly wild, she thought. Like a bear who'd tucked himself into a collared shirt.

His own hands were clutching pieces of garbage too. "Does *anybody* work here?"

//

Sonia didn't mind her own past. After all, it had brought her to Victor. And for the most part Victor seemed to feel the same way. They kept their former selves to themselves and lived in the present as best they could. But today the past was rising.

Sonia's bags were packed, waiting by the door. She'd begun feeling better as the evening came on, having worried all afternoon about leaving town in the middle of a fight. And now, as she sat down with him at the dining room table to talk about the papers, he'd asked the question again.

"This again?" she said. "Seriously?"

"Yes," said Victor. "This. Again."

"Nothing ever happened," Sonia assured him. "He was just a little creepy."

"You think?"

"How long are you going to obsess over this?"

"You said he put his hands on you. Like how exactly? Like he put his hand in your hand? Like a handshake?"

Sonia tilted her head. "Now you're being naïve."

"I'm trying not to be."

"We were kids," she said, as if being a child were the same as being a victim. She thought of the papers upstairs in the extra bedroom. They were supposed to be talking about finalizing the adoption. Sonia had already filled out most of it, and now, while she was at Allie's, it would give Victor time to finish his sections.

"He'd pat our knees," she added. "Touch our hair. That sort of thing."

"Your sister's hair too?"

"*My* hair," Sonia said. "Girls deal with that sort of stuff. Weird uncles and all. Mr. Bello wasn't a pedophile, he was our handyman."

Victor leaned back into his chair with arms crossed. "More like a *handsy*-man."

"You're punning now? I thought this was honestly bothering you."

"It is. And I'm saying I'd like to do something about it."

"Well, Mr. Bello's like seventy-five years old," she said. "And he's in the middle of wallpapering my parents' dining room right now so you might think twice about how pissed my mother will be if you interrupt the project with your righteous indignation."

"Now who's joking around?"

"You're not a crime boss, Victor. You can't go breaking an old man's legs because he patted my thigh thirty years ago."

Victor's brow scrunched. "Who says I'm a crime boss?"

"You tell that story to *every*body, hon."

"It's a good story." His voice rose defensively. "And besides, I tell it with self-deprecation. Don't I?"

Sonia moved around the corner of the table, sat sideways in his lap, and put her arms around his neck.

"You know," he said in a less aggrieved voice, his fingers touching a button on her yellow blouse, "I did move a lot of stolen goods that summer."

She kissed him on the forehead, craning her neck to settle against the stubbled warmth of his face. "Of course you did, Don Corleone. Tell me the story again."

And he did tell it again, the summer job he'd had during college, unwittingly employed by one of the stale mob outfits outside the city. He'd spent the summer driving a truck between a secondhand store in Chicago and a warehouse in Triton. And it *was* a pretty good story, she had to admit. When he'd still been with Scanlan Chemical and there'd been parties at the house full of scientists and engineers who knew him as one of their own, it was endearing to hear that kind of tale—a chemical engineering student moonlighting for the mob. But ever since Victor bought the cemetery and changed careers, his audience of co-workers had turned coarser, more readily believing in the story's criminal embellishments. The truth was, he'd not known at the time that he was transporting stolen goods, not until years later when "Uncle" Mel got arrested in a mob sting. And while the scientists and engineers had been willing to suspend their disbelief in order to indulge a good yarn, these cemetery employees—the oddball administrative staffers, the teenage part-timers, the gravediggers—had listened to Victor tell the story at last winter's Christmas party with such credulous looks on their faces, as if, in the normal course of a life, a person couldn't be expected *not* to have dabbled in criminal enterprise. But also there was something about Victor, too, these days, which made the story so plausible—his unshaven face, his dirt-smeared coveralls—as though he'd just come back from burying a body. Which of course he had.

Sonia didn't love it, this new career of his—the money being less, the hours longer—but she did appreciate that Victor was made happier by it. For a long time he'd liked chemical engineering, and now, for these five years, he'd loved running a small-town cemetery. He liked digging up the earth and worrying over the trees. He liked staying late to scare off the high school kids who came to desecrate a haunted grave. Most of all, though, he liked that his mother lay under the ground there.

Publicly, he claimed he bought Oak Hill because his high school chemistry teacher was buried there, but Sonia tried to make it known that he'd actually wanted to clean up the final resting place of his mother. Friends of theirs had had questions when he so abruptly quit Scanlan. Friends of hers, really. Victor was likable enough—crassly funny when he was up to it, a brooding teddy bear when he wasn't—but he'd kept no real friendships in his own life.

"His mother died when he was young," Sonia would sometimes explain in an effort to humanize her husband. People struggled to see beyond the tobacco bulge in his cheek, or the way he'd pop up around town dirt-stained and smelling of fertilizer. "And he never even met his father," she would add, making the story into an orphan's tale.

"Abandonment issues," a friend had recently replied. "I see. Is that why he has such a hard time letting things go?"

Sonia didn't usually address follow-up questions, not wanting to stoke curiosity after all. She knew her husband's heart better than his mind, and it was heart that mattered. The truth of Victor Senn was that he'd come to prefer the simple worth of putting shovel to soil over a well-compensated career in a laboratory. So she brushed off such questions, usually with more humanizing statements. "He worries over those oak trees like you wouldn't believe!"

But when, in these hours before Sonia was to visit her sister for the night, Victor became so suddenly curious about her past, she felt as if some unspoken line item in their marital contract was being breached.

"What about you?" Sonia was still on his lap, but she'd straightened her torso, holding herself at arm's length. "It's not like I ever get stories about *your* childhood."

He looked up into his brow. "Okay," he said. "You want to hear about *my* handyman when I was a boy?"

"You're teasing me." She closed her mouth tight and leveled her eyelids in such a way that he might understand she sometimes required sincerity. "Okay, so you actually had a handyman," she said cautiously. "Okay, I'm believing you here. I'm trusting you."

"He fixed things," Victor said. "But he was like a nanny too."

"A manny," she said.

"Now *you're* punning."

"A handy-manny!"

Victor didn't speak.

"You're making this up," she said.

"I'm not."

She held out her pinkie. "Swear?"

He hooked her finger with his own. "This was in middle school," he began, "in the group home. The foster parents in this place were just running a scam to collect government checks. They were never there. They'd hire women to watch the house, but these were people who couldn't even speak English. It was chaos at that place, so these women were always walking off the job. Then one day, this guy came over to install a padlock on the fridge. He had one of those work shirts with the cursive stitching above the pocket—Roman was his name—and of course the foster mom lady convinced him to hang out awhile longer until she got back from the store. Just like that, he became the new babysitter."

"There was a lock on the fridge?" Sonia said. "You poor thing."

"No embellishments, please. This is my story."

"Sorry."

"Roman would keep us busy with experiments, like citric acid and baking soda explosions, toilet cleaner bombs, that sort of thing. It really put the hook in me, you know, the chemistry involved. I think maybe he'd been a science teacher wherever he'd been from."

"Was he from Romania?"

"More jokes?"

"I'm shutting up now."

"That's okay," he said. "That was the end of my story."

"No it wasn't."

"It was," he said.

"Victor . . ."

He watched her wait, his eyes blinking. "That's it. Really. It was a long time ago. I remember he had really big hands. And these wooden, old-world tools. Is that enough? Aren't you supposed to be heading off to Allie's?"

"I've got time."

"Your sister's gonna call here any minute and yell at me, you know."

She unlaced her fingers from behind his neck and put her hands in her own lap. "Keep going."

"There were times," he said, "when the foster parents would leave town and he'd stay overnight with us and sort of stand guard in the hallway, pacing back and forth between our bedrooms. All night long you'd hear him coming and going, the wooden tools on his belt clacking together."

"And . . . ?"

"And what?"

"What did he do then?" Sonia asked.

"I think his family must've been taken away by secret police or something, to be that paranoid." Victor shrugged. "Anyway, that was Roman. Later he died. He's actually in my cemetery now."

"That's it?"

"You haven't exactly gone on and on about *your* handyman."

"There was nothing to tell!" she shouted, but then she thought of him, of Mr. Bello. He entered her mind suddenly, with a raw clarity that hadn't been there before. Not the addled old man she'd seen as recently as last month fixing a downspout on her parents' house, but the stocky middle-aged man of her youth, pausing in his repair of the playroom radiator to adjust himself beneath his work smock.

Hours ago she'd referred to her parents' "perverted old handyman," and ever since, Victor had been demanding more information. At first, her husband's concern had seemed almost selfish, like a ridiculous jealousy at not having married her soon enough. "I meant to say 'creepy,'" she'd added at dinner, "not 'perverted.'" But he'd brought it up again and again, and each time he did she felt his concern for the young girl she'd once been morphing into something more like a mistrust of her present self. Simple jealousy after all. But it wasn't that. It couldn't be. In all the world Victor seemed to trust *only* Sonia. So she tried to be casual about it, changing the subject, cracking a joke. Let Victor see her total lack of concern and relocate his compass in time.

"Raymond Bello," Victor said, as if spitting the man's name. "There's something you're not saying."

Another memory rose and crystallized, an image of his hands—too soft for a tradesman—adjusting the hem of Sonia's Sunday dress in the moment before her father hobbled into the kitchen. The handyman had always been around in that way, living above the garage, roaming the house at will, always fixing the playroom radiator (broken again!), always smoothing blouse wrinkles and plucking stray hairs off shoulders.

"Is this how you're going to be with a child?" she asked. "Endless interrogation over spilled milk? Jesus, Victor, we're not running a group home here. Sometimes you've got to let things go."

He straightened, dumping her onto her feet so he could walk to the other side of the room to face her from a greater distance. "You're always pressing me to be serious," he said, "but I've been asking you one simple question and you've done nothing but dodge the answer."

She wanted to make a point here—the irony of Victor Senn accusing someone else of being flippant and evasive—but it would serve no purpose beyond raising again the notion that she was becoming too much like him. Victor didn't mind being Victor, but he didn't want to rub off on anyone else. It was why he didn't keep friends. She'd seen how, at social gatherings, people would listen to him with a sort of disturbed reverence, how they'd adopt his crass expressions into their own language. It must've been why he loved Sonia, his opposite in so many ways—younger than him, popular, religious, firmly possessed of her own separate personality.

She wanted to say some of these things to him now, but he was already out the door, off on one of his walks. She moved to the window and watched him stride down the block toward Oak Hill, the low August sun crashing in the west. He'd go wash the trucks or sharpen the landscaping tools, and eventually he'd come home ready to apologize, to accept apologies.

This was how their marriage worked. They kept to themselves mostly, loved and trusted mostly. And when occasionally something ugly came between them, one of them walked it off while the other cleaned the house. And later, they always put it to rest. They'd cook a meal together, drink a good bottle of wine, go to bed. He'd move his mouth over her body beneath the covers, she'd turn and loosen in forgiveness. In the morning they'd go to her church, then his diner.

But that would need to be tomorrow. Today they had to speed up the process somehow. She was supposed to have left for Allie's house an hour ago.

//

As she got out of the shower, she heard a noise below the window, someone coughing out on the sidewalk, spitting. She dressed quickly and went downstairs. A red shape wavered behind the front door's frosted-glass inset.

When she opened the door, a man in camel-colored work

pants and a red sweatshirt stood on the stoop with a large de-
flated duffel bag on his shoulder.

"Long-Lived Removal Services," the stranger announced.
As he extended his hand, his slender forearm telescoped out of
the thick cuff of his sleeve, pale and bony.

She looked past him, still thinking it was supposed to have
been her husband. "Can I help you?"

The sun had set and the sky smoldered behind him, his
face a shadowed blur in the foreground. He finally withdrew
his unshaken hand, pulling a binder from his bag, and leaning
forward into the brighter light coming out the doorway. The
binder's cover had a picture of the grim reaper holding a chain
saw. "That's a bit dramatic," he said, apologetically. Then he
flipped pages forward and tapped a picture of a beetle.

"Oak slayers," Sonia said.

"*Agrilus quercata,*" he pronounced with flourish. He sighed,
then coughed. He hiked his duffel bag higher on his shoulder
and stepped forward.

"You're coming in then," Sonia said, swinging backward
with the door as the man pressed into the house. "It's Victor
you want to speak with, but he's at—"

The man shuffled past her, through the entryway and into
the living room.

"I was saying that my husband's the one who runs the cemetery, so you'll want to come back when—" Sonia watched him
sit down on the couch. He pulled out a bandana and coughed
into it, the tendons in his neck standing up as he wheezed.

She said, "Can I get you some water?"

The man didn't answer. He busied himself setting his binder
out on the coffee table, rifling through his big bag.

When she came back from the kitchen, he took the water

from her, gasping as he swallowed, then set the empty glass on the coffee table.

"Is this about an order Victor already placed?" Sonia asked, taking a seat across from him. "Or, I'm sorry, what is it you're selling exactly?"

"They're coming," he said, tapping the picture of the beetle, then turning to a page with a spreadsheet of tree names, heights, prices.

"Victor's trees are still healthy," she said.

A broad grin bent across the man's face. "But for how long?" he asked, flipping now to a page full of chemical names, capacities, prices. He had the air of a con man, she thought, pushy and polite at once. How had she let him inside her home so easily? She thought of the adoption papers on the comforter upstairs in the spare bedroom. A proxy for the child they might someday put in that very bed. What kind of mother lets a stranger into the house while the baby is napping? What kind of father invites a con man over to begin with?

"Did you say that Victor *asked* you to come here?"

"I can see the future, Miss Senn." He put his pale eyes on her directly. "Your husband's oak trees will be dead in three years."

Sonia picked up his empty water glass and motioned to her suitcase by the door. "I'm afraid I'm leaving town, so you'll have to come back when Victor's here." She stood up, but he didn't stand with her. He was digging inside his bag again, bringing out a slender glass vial. He held the tube out horizontally for her to see the living insect contained within. As he tilted the vial back and forth between them, his colorless eyes warped and twisted behind the glass.

"In life," he said, "we don't usually get to see the trouble coming." He unscrewed the top of the vial and dumped the silver beetle onto the coffee table, then took the empty glass from Sonia's hand and turned it over to trap the creature inside.

She glanced at the door, desperate now to have her husband back, to offer him apologies for what she'd said. Just her own reservations about motherhood, she'd tell him. *Look at how easily I let this strange man into our house!* She thought of Bello then, his fleshy hand up under her hair, the warm pads of his fingers on the back of her neck as she'd hunched over a work sheet. The stranger on her couch didn't look dangerous at all, and this fact made her suddenly afraid.

"I have to go," she said, thrusting her hand out to end things with a shake.

The man's head hung low, wagging slightly as he made a *tsk*ing sound, until finally he'd urged the insect back into the vial. When the cap was on again, air began flowing back into Sonia's lungs. Then a shape appeared in the opaque glass of the door, footsteps scraping up the front walk.

Something flooded into Sonia then, relief and panic at once. She stood there, frozen by it, her hand still levered out toward the stranger, with the soft shape of her husband growing larger in the clouded glass. But the panic kept flooding in, as if these were the most precarious moments of a prisoner exchange or a hostage release, as if she'd let a killer into her home, or a kidnapper, the child they'd not yet had in such danger.

"I really do have to go," she repeated.

Then her balance disappeared, and the stranger's hands were wrapped around her own as he hauled himself up off the couch. "Yes," he said, not yet letting go, holding her gaze with his empty white eyes, his crooked grin, his dry bony hands around her own. "Yes, you do have to go."

The door opened and Victor stepped inside.

"This man came to speak to you about your trees." Sonia felt breathless, harried. *There's a killer in the house,* she wanted to scream. *There's an oak slayer in his bag.* "But he was just leaving."

"My trees?" Victor asked.

"But he's already on his way," she insisted.

The stranger set his bag down again. He took his binder back out. He said, "Ma'am, would it be too much to ask for one more glass of water?"

As Sonia entered the kitchen, her phone was buzzing on the counter.

"Tell me you're not still at *home*?" her sister whined on the other end of the line.

"I'm waylaid, Al. Something's come up."

"Come on, Sonia, we're entitled to a girls' night out."

"I'm hurrying, Allie."

"Well, hurry faster."

Sonia hung up.

In the living room, the men were sitting. Victor leaned forward, staring at the glass vial. He said, "Three years?"

"I can see the future," the stranger said.

Sonia's cell phone buzzed again. Allie. Ignore. She brought the water glasses out into the living room and set them on the coffee table.

The stranger was saying, ". . . In life we don't usually get to see the—" Then he turned abruptly to Sonia. "Am I delaying your wife's departure?"

"Give me a moment." Victor rose and ushered Sonia back into the kitchen.

"I'm really sorry," Sonia whispered. "He just invited himself in."

"It's okay," said Victor.

"I'm calling Allie to cancel."

Victor took her phone. "Don't do that. We're fine."

She lowered her voice even further. "I'm freaked out, Victor."

"Why, what happened?"

"I just have this awful feeling."

"It was only a fight," he said. "It's over. I'm sorry. You're sorry. Come home tomorrow and we'll drink wine together."

"Tomorrow—"

The phone buzzed in Victor's hand. Sonia could hear her sister's voice.

"I'm not *holding* her here, Allie." Victor rolled his eyes. "I thought the show doesn't start until ten. Okay, okay. She's getting into the car right now. Yeah, I get it, great seats. She's on her way. Bye."

"That man is *strange*," Sonia whispered. "Don't let him kidnap you or anything."

"What?"

"And don't drink your water."

"*What?*"

"I can't remember which glass is which. Don't drink either." She looked at her husband desperately. She felt desperate. She couldn't say why, except that her breathing wouldn't calm and the stranger's waxy handshake still clung to her flesh. "Victor . . ." she began. There seemed to be more to say. "Tomorrow . . ." she began again.

But her husband only smiled, tender and patronizing, and said, "Would you get out of here already?"

//

Outside, full dark had fallen over Wicklow and it seemed too late all of a sudden. A light rain spat on the windshield. Inside the car, Sonia felt vaguely surreptitious, as if she were leaving Victor for good. This is how it would feel, she thought. A bag of clothes on the passenger seat, a sister on the other end of the highway making up a spare bedroom. As she backed down the driveway, the sensation intensified. This is what life was like without children. You had only one person to betray in order to cut yourself loose. She thought of Allie's two girls, of her husband, Andrew, of the way, whenever they went out together, Allie would drink too much and say, "I love Andrew, I do, but if we didn't have kids I honestly don't know whether I'd go home to him tonight."

This was the relief of having no children, and the terror too. A car ride was never just a car ride. It was a test of your commitment to the man you found yourself constantly trying to rationalize to others. Trying to humanize. Maybe she *was* leaving him, for a night anyway. And tomorrow she would reassess things honestly. Tonight she would go out and speak like Allie spoke. *I love Victor,* she'd say, *but I honestly don't know if I can continue to put up with his abandonment issues.* And tomorrow she'd wake up and say to herself: *You don't have to go back if you don't want to.*

She said these words aloud now, in the car. She was on the highway already. She was merging onto the tollway, bending around the city. The sun disappeared and the darkness came on. She dug her cell phone from her purse.

"I'm freaking out, Allie."

The other end of the line was cluttered with background noise. The twins were singing in British accents, over a clanking sound. "Traffic," Allie said. "You should've left an hour ago."

"Traffic's okay," said Sonia. "It's other stuff."

The background clanking grew louder, higher pitched, like a wrench on pipe. "Andrew's got a secret route I bet. I can call him and ask—"

"It's Victor."

"Hold on," Allie said, muffling the phone. "Girls," she shouted, "it's called dress-up, not dress-down."

The clanking stopped.

"What's going on over there?" Sonia asked.

"My girls watch one music video and their hoopskirts turn into hooker wear."

The background noise was gone entirely now. A widening, anxious silence.

One of the twins could be heard asking what hooker wear was.

"It means put your clothes back on," Allie said. "Mr. Bello doesn't want to see your underwear."

The clanking resumed abruptly.

"Allie . . . ?" Sonia said.

"Girls, seriously, get your pajamas on. Aunt Sonia's going to be here soon."

"Allie . . . ?"

The phone unmuffled and her sister came back on. "It's that British singer, what's her name, the one who's always getting out of limos without any panties. Honestly, it's impossible to shield your kids from all this—"

"Is he there right now?" Sonia asked. "Mr. Bello?"

"Mom sent him over. He's fixing the radiator. If I need to meet you there, he can watch the girls until Andrew gets back from—"

Sonia ditched her cell phone onto the passenger seat. Her

foot grew heavy on the accelerator. A truck fell past on the right and shrank in the rearview. The speedometer needle traced an arc over the top of the dial. Seventy-five, eighty, eighty-five. The car struggled to find more power. The dashboard hummed. She wove around a van full of elderly people, a red sports car, a motorcycle. Someone honked. She put the wipers on. She put more weight on the pedal, thinking hard about the past, about the movements of Bello's hands, the way he would hold one so gently inside the other, then switch, and back again, as if wringing them, or keeping them occupied lest they wander. She drifted right and roared up the off-ramp into Tower Hill, whipping through the darkened downtown full of banks and boutiques. Just a mile now from Allie's kids, just a minute—when a light changed color and a car appeared and the world suddenly turned over and her teeth all came loose at once and she thought of herself at that age, of Bello tending a fresh scrape on her knee, his free hand sliding up her thigh as she'd wept. She remembered thinking he was almost handsome underneath the soft fat, that he was probably very sorry for having done it just then, brief as it was. She'd seen, in that moment, the self-hate of a grown man who knew better but still couldn't not reach the extra inch. Just to know he'd gone for it the once was probably enough for him to never go again. He'd certainly recoiled from her, from what he'd been trying to do to her, and it was then that she'd felt a wave of sympathy for the man, not so ugly with his glasses off, his big soft hand pinching the bridge of his nose. "It's okay," she'd said to him, thinking she'd rather save him than ruin him further. He was already ruined, it seemed. "It's okay."

Is this it, she thought. Is this how I die? In an overturned car on the run from my husband? There were children to save, weren't there? Bottles of wine to drink? There were forms to fill and an orphan to adopt. There were days and years left to explain her marriage to people who lack imagination.

She opened her mouth to argue a different outcome, to claim a different fate, but no sound came out. Her cheeks felt ripped, her face hot and welling. A man had crawled halfway into the broken passenger window. Someone else's husband. Someone else's ongoing rationalization. "It's okay," he said. "Don't move. I've called an ambulance. I'll stay here with you." His breath was scotch, but she didn't blame him for it. The red light had been hers, if memory served. For as long as memory would serve. She only wanted to explain to him her unfinished errand. She tried to speak again, but the memory of what she'd wanted to say was already skating away. An innocence had been at stake, or its loss was to be mourned. To look at the desperate face hanging off the man inside her car, it seemed that too much had happened already. To hear his sorrowful chanting—*I'm here with you . . . I'm here with you . . .* —was to understand that there was absolutely no going back. She closed her eyes and tried to think what it was she'd needed to say, but nothing would take full shape inside her head. Just hands without minds controlling them and errands unfinished, half a man shouting encouragement into an upside-down car. *Where is your other half,* she wanted to ask him. *Where is mine?* His hands grew dark and the streetlamps dimmed, her vision closing down. Until there was only the sound of the half-man's chant, a tender song to carry her off, a final petition for the one thing we all want.

ACKNOWLEDGMENTS

Thanks to Robert Guinsler, who, excepting only my family, is owed the most. To Sarah Goldberg, whose guidance on this project made every page better. And to David Lamb for giving the manuscript a chance to begin with.

Thanks to Brady Udall for letting me into class. To Janet Desaulniers for letting me into school. And in particular to Jim McManus for a decade's worth of writing advice, career perspective, and friendship without which I would be in another line of work entirely.

Thanks to Bradley Greenburg for crucial help with this manuscript. To Natalie Danford, Tonaya Thompson, Linda Swanson-Davies, and Susan Burmeister-Brown, who helped publish several of these stories before there was a book to put them in.

A not-small debt of gratitude is owed to the grandparents of my children—to Wendy and Michael Chance, to Cathy and Jim Nowacki—for granting me the time to write many of these stories in the first place. And to Garnet and Bon, during whose regular naps the rest of the book was written.

Finally, at the risk of undermining all gratitude so far described, this is Anastasia's book. She is its muse, its sponsor, and its original editor. She is its therapist and enabler both, and the first person, myself included, who thought I should write it. If the preceding fifty thousand words has been an attempt on my part to sound clever or artful, I submit this last sentence as a direct item. This book is for Anastasia.

ABOUT THE AUTHOR

Baird Harper's fiction has appeared in *Glimmer Train, Tin House, StoryQuarterly,* and the *Chicago Tribune.* His stories have been anthologized in the 2009 and 2010 editions of *Best New American Voices, 40 Years of CutBank,* and *New Stories from the Midwest 2016,* and have won the 2014 Raymond Carver Short Story Contest and the 2010 Nelson Algren Literary Award. He teaches writing at Loyola University and the University of Chicago.